MAIL ORDER

Melody

BRIDES OF SEATTLE – BOOK 5

CYNTHIA WOOLF

Books by Cynthia Woolf

BRIDES OF SEATTLE
Mail Order Mystery
Mail Order Mayhem
Mail Order Mix-Up
Mail Order Moonlight
Mail Order Melody

CENTRAL CITY BRIDES
The Dancing Bride
The Sapphire Bride
The Irish Bride
The Pretender Bride

MONTANA SKY WORLD
A Family for Christmas
Kissed by a Stranger
Thorpe's Mail-Order Bride

HOPE'S CROSSING
The Hunter Bride
The Replacement Bride
The Stolen Bride
The Unexpected Bride

AMERICAN MAIL-ORDER BRIDES
Genevieve, Bride of Nevada

THE SURPRISE BRIDES
Gideon

PROLOGUE

November 15, 1864, New Bedford, Massachusetts
Hall of the Presbyterian Church

"Hi, ladies. I'm Adam Talbot. It's my job to explain to you what will happen when we leave here." He looked around the room at all the eager faces. His sister Suzanne had arranged for the hall to be used and all the chairs to be brought in. "From the looks of this turnout, we'll be heading to Seattle in the Washington Territory in about a month. That should give you time to settle your affairs and be ready to depart on December fifteenth. Is there anyone here who cannot make that deadline?"

At first no one spoke up, and then a hand was tentatively lifted. The woman was striking with black hair, pale skin, dark blue eyes and a firm jut of her chin.

1

"Yes, Miss, what is your question?"

She stood. "My son will not be released from school by that time. They don't get out until the twentieth."

"You have children?" asked Adam.

"She's got children," whispered a blonde woman behind the speaker.

"Who in their right mind," said another woman farther back in the room. "Would take children on this trip?"

The woman standing looked around defiantly, her eyes narrowed and her mouth in a thin line.

All the other women were silenced by her expression.

"Yes," her attention back on Adam. "You didn't say we couldn't have children, only that we were not currently married to anyone. Well, I'm not married any longer and I have two children."

Adam ran his hand behind his neck and looked over at Jason. "I don't know. I...uh, Jason."

"What?" Jason turned from talking to their brother Drew.

Adam pointed at the woman with the raven hair, standing now with her hands folded demurely in front of her. "This lady has children."

The woman directed her attention toward Jason. Her back must have had a steel rod up it because Adam was sure he'd never seen anyone with such stiff posture.

"That's right I do, Mr. Talbot. Two of them. Before you say I can't go, you should know that I'm a qualified mid-wife, almost a doctor. I didn't quite finish my college education because I got married. I needed only to complete my thesis. When these ladies get married, babies are the next to come." She lifted an eyebrow. "You'll need me."

"Well, Miss—" said Jason.

"It's Mrs. Martell. Karen Martell."

"Well, Mrs. Martell, you're quite right. We will need your services. I suggest you withdraw your children a little early from school."

"I have only one child in school, my son, Larry. He's in first grade."

Jason cocked his head to one side and narrowed his eyes. "At such a young age, leaving school five days early will not hurt him and you know that. What is really your problem, Mrs. Martell?"

Adam thought Jason was being a bit harsh, but understood the need for the information from the woman.

"I really wanted to know what you would say about children coming. There are many widows with children who are seeking new husbands."

Adam nodded, afraid the answer would limit the number of women to accompany them to Seattle. "I understand your concern. With a few exceptions, we prefer women without children. We can't guarantee they'll find husbands if they have children. Many men do not want a ready-made family. Others won't mind at all but we can't say which will and which won't."

The woman nodded.

"I understand but I believe you are making a mistake."

"Mrs. Martell," said Adam. "There will always be exceptions and you are one. We'd like for you to accompany us to Seattle."

She smiled, radiantly.

"Thank you. We'll be ready on the fifteenth," She sat but the smile never left her face.

"Good." Adam cocked an eyebrow. "*Very good.*"

Karen still smiled after she'd reseated herself. Adam Talbot was a very handsome man. If she were honest with herself, all of the Talbots were quite good looking, but something about Adam drew her.

She glanced up and was startled, yet at the same time pleased, to find him staring at her. Karen quickly shifted her gaze down but continued to smile.

In no way could she become involved with him, or anyone else. She still loved Douglas, who she'd seen last just twenty-one months ago. She didn't know at the time that she was pregnant or that in less than a month she'd be a widow. Patty was born on August 24, 1863.

The Union won the battle, but the cost had been high. The confederates lost over 11,000 men in the three-day exchange, according to the soldiers who came to tell her about Douglas.

Karen had been heartbroken and only in the last month or so had started wearing any clothing that wasn't black. She needed to find work and that wouldn't happen here. Seattle was a new frontier. She needed to make this move for her children and, if she was honest, for herself.

She missed adult conversation. Though she appreciated the time with her children, the money was nearly gone and becoming a mail-order bride seemed to be the answer to a prayer.

As a medically trained midwife she was prepared to attend and treat the women who were to become brides and would likely be having children fairly shortly thereafter. If she was part of this group, she had a built-in clientele. She'd only needed one more semester to graduate, but Douglas wanted a wife who stayed home and took care of the house and children.

Karen glanced up at the podium. Jason, who she assumed was the eldest brother since he did most of the talking, told them when and where to meet. Her gaze wandered to Adam, who still looked her way.

She quickly glanced at Jason and paid attention to what he was saying. They would leave from the docks on December fifteenth. She would be ready to leave her old life behind, but was she prepared for what lay ahead?

CHAPTER 1

March 6, 1866

Karen gazed out her kitchen window, still awed by the majestic Cascade Mountains in the distance. The setting sun made their snowcapped peaks sparkle like diamonds.

On the other side of the house she saw the waters of Puget Sound roiling with the March winds blowing over them. Adam Talbot crowded her thoughts, as he often did when she was alone.

I've been in Seattle nearly a year and Adam isn't any more friendly than he was on the ship here. He avoided me then and has been avoiding me since. So far I've delivered four babies from the marriages that have taken place. There are four women pregnant, including Rachel and Lucy Talbot. They are so obviously in love with their husbands.

But Adam doesn't seem interested in me and he's the only one I'm interested in getting to know. I'll concentrate on my medical practice and then I'll forget him.

She walked to the children's room. Alice was still there having watched the children all day and had just put the children down for the night. Getting Patty to sleep was getting harder since Karen's grandmother's music box had stopped working. Now no songs played to provide a *melody* to sing to, since the box broke.

A knock sounded on the door and Alice left to see who was calling at such a time. Karen wasn't surprised. She was called on at all hours to deliver babies.

Alice tapped the door to the children's bedroom.

"Karen? Adam Talbot is here. He said Rachel is having her baby and you should come right away."

Karen went to her bedroom, picked her Gladstone bag off the floor and her shawl off her bed. *I shouldn't be excited to spend time with Adam he's usually so standoffish and proper. If he would be friendlier...* She sighed. *Oh, well. It will probably be a quiet ride.*

Alice waited in the hall outside the bedroom. Standing there in her pink dress, holding the lamp, her blonde hair shining in the flickering light, Karen wondered why the woman hadn't found a man to marry. Of course, many people probably wondered the same thing about Karen.

"I just put the kids down for the night. Will you keep an eye on them while I'm gone?"

Alice nodded. "Of course. Now go and send word when Rachel has the baby."

"I'll be back soon thereafter with the news."

Karen walked out to the front porch where Adam waited. Even in the low light he was the most handsome man she'd ever known. Her heart beat faster whenever he was near.

"Good evening, Adam."

"Hello, Karen. May I take your case for you?"

She handed him the bag. "Please."

Their hands touched for just a moment and she was warmed to the core. Even Douglas had never given her that feeling.

Her gaze flashed to Adam.

His eyes were wide, and he smiled. "Well," was all he said before holding out his arm for her.

She slipped her hand through the crook in his elbow, and they descended the stairs to the buggy parked on the street in front of the small clapboard house that was her home. They'd had rain, so the street was muddy, but Adam had pulled the buggy as close to the porch as possible for her. His thoughtfulness pleased her.

He set the bag in the back seat.

"Let me help you. No need for you to get muddy when I already am."

He swung her up into his arms and carried her to the surrey.

"Oh, my." She wrapped her arms around his neck, enjoying the sensation of being carried by a strong lumberjack. His scent surrounded her, sandalwood, pine and man.

Her head told her that she shouldn't enjoy it too much, that he wasn't interested in her, but her heart still held out hope.

Setting her safely in the front seat, he then walked around the back and slid into the seat beside her.

He picked up the reins. "Are you ready?"

"Yes."

Adam clicked his teeth and swatted the reins down on the horse's rump. "Giddy up."

The horse took off at a fast walk. When they reached the edge of town, he slapped its rear end again.

The beautiful black stallion was the same one that Adam usually rode. The animal trotted up the hill to the Talbot home.

"How long has Rachel been having pain?"

"A long time. About six hours or so. At least that's when Jason told us and began to prowl the living room."

"I'd guess she's been in labor much longer, but she probably didn't tell anyone." Karen calculated that Rachel could have been in labor for twelve to eighteen hours by now and could very well be ready to deliver the child.

He shrugged. "Maybe. I don't know much about having babies. Billy and the puppies born after

Jason and Rachel brought Lucky home are my only reference."

She smiled. "That's not very much experience, since having puppies and having babies are very different." She took a deep breath of the air scented by the evergreen forest they drove through. The crisp, cold air seemed to make the pine aroma crisper and seem cleaner. Looking up the stars sparkled as bright as any diamond she'd ever seen.

He glanced at her. "Yes, ma'am they are. I'd have to say I'm blissfully ignorant."

"Well, for Rachel's sake, I'm glad I'm not."

"Me, too."

Karen put a hand on his arm. "I know Jason is worried sick that he'll lose her like he did Cassie, his first wife. But Rachel is very strong and I can think of no reason anything will go wrong. I'm very sure everything will be fine."

"I hope so. I don't think Jason could go through that again."

"Trust me, when I say Rachel will be all right."

"I do. Trust you, I mean."

Karen smiled, pleased that he had faith in her.

He pulled the horse to a stop in front of the three story log house. It was the largest home in Seattle. Adam set the brake before jumping down and running around to help Karen down.

She smoothed her skirt while he got her bag from the back seat and then they both hurried up the porch steps and into the house.

Jason walked over as soon as she entered the living room.

"Karen! I'm so glad you're here."

He took her hand and practically dragged her to the stairs directly across the living room from the entry door.

"Jason." She pulled back on her hand and made him stop. She glanced around and saw all of his brothers, his sister-in-law Josie, and all of the children were waiting for the birth with him. "Jason. Slow down. I know the way to the bedroom and can walk up the stairs myself."

"Of course, you do." Jason ran his hands through his dark brown hair, leaving bits of it standing on end and making him look rather unhinged. "I'm sorry. I'm a bit crazy with worry for her." His voice turned into a whisper. "I couldn't bear it if I lost her."

Her throat tightened and she fought back tears. She knew exactly how he felt because she had lost Douglas and it nearly killed her. Taking his hand, she squeezed it. "You won't. Trust me and let me do my job."

Jason took a deep breath. "All right. Go. Let me know if you need anything at all."

She placed a hand on the railing, and then turned back toward Jason. "Is Lucy with her?"

"Yes," answered Drew, the youngest Talbot brother and Lucy's husband. "She's been with her all afternoon. I'm not sure seeing what Rachel is going through is good for Lucy, since our baby is due in a month or so."

Karen smiled. She had lots of experience dealing with nervous fathers. She let go of the railing and patted Drew's shoulder. "Lucy's fine. She'll have more knowledge and know not to be afraid. That's a good thing."

He shook his head and ran his hand behind his neck. "If you say so. I worry she'll be afraid after she sees what Rachel is going through."

"Trust me. She'll be fine. I'll need her help and keeping her busy will keep her mind off of what's happening until the baby gets here. Then I'll have her clean up the babe before giving him...or her, to Rachel. Now if you'll excuse me, I'll go see my patient."

"I'm coming with you. I need to know she's all right," said Jason. "I've been down here too long."

"All right, but stay up by the headboard and out of my way. Understand?" *I'm not sure how smart it is to let him stay, but given his past, he needs to see her be well.*

"Yes, ma'am."

Karen and Jason entered the room just as Rachel, sweating and pale, moaned through a particularly bad pain.

"Good evening, my sweet friends. What have we got going on here? I heard through the grapevine that we're having a baby and darn if that doesn't appear to be the case," Karen quipped.

"Stop trying to be funny, Karen," snapped Rachel lying on the bed, her beautiful blonde hair stuck to her cheek. "Just get this baby out of me."

"All right. Let me look and see where we are in this process."

Karen washed her hands and then pulled forceps from her bag before she examined Rachel. "Oh, my. Looks like I got here just in time. You're further along than I thought you'd be. It looks like this little one is ready to come out. He's starting to crown." Karen straightened to address Rachel directly. "How long have you been in labor?"

Rachel huffed out a breath. "Since last night, but then they were only small pains, nothing big."

Karen set out her instruments on the bed. "Even small pains count as labor. With the big pains, we say you're in hard labor or the beginning of hard labor. Since the baby is crowning, I want you to push. Jason, if you want to stay, let her hold your hands for support. I'm glad you put down the oil cloth or you'd have to get rid of the mattress. Ready?" Rachel lay on the bed, Jason at the headboard holding her hands. Karen laid down a towel to catch the baby and the fluids as much as possible. Then she had to pull up her skirt to climb onto the foot of the bed. "Push. I want you to put your hands on your belly and tighten those muscles as much as you can. Okay, push now with all your might. Tighten those muscles. Harder. Push."

Rachel pushed and bore down. "I can't push anymore."

"All right. Rest a moment." Karen put her stethoscope on Rachel's belly, listened for the baby's heart beat. It was strong. Unbidden, the memory of the baby she lost assaulted her. She pushed it from her mind and concentrated on Rachel. She would not lose another baby.

After several sessions of pushing and resting, Rachel was exhausted. She flopped back against the pillows. "I'm so tired."

"I know, but you need to give another push. This time make it absolutely as hard as you can." Karen was poised to catch the babe as it entered the world.

"Come on, love, you can do it." Jason stood near Rachel's head. He held her hand, and she squeezed his hand until his knuckles went white, which was good.

He stayed up there and out of Karen's way. She was glad for the emotional support he gave to Rachel. The ordeal was easier on her with him near. "Okay, here we go with one last hard push. Give me all you've got."

Rachel screamed as she pushed, the slimy baby came into the world.

"Well," Rachel asked, leaning on propped elbows. "What is it? Boy or girl?"

Karen smiled. "I'll have to stop saying his and start saying hers. You have a beautiful baby girl. Let Lucy get her cleaned up."

Karen checked for any outward abnormalities, and then she held the baby upside down, cleaned out her mouth and felt to make sure the roof of her mouth was solid. Once her mouth was clear, the infant gave a small cry which echoed through the silent room.

Karen then handed the baby to Lucy, who bathed and clothed her.

"Here you go, Karen. All ready for Mama."

Lucy handed the crying baby, dressed in a diaper and thin gown, swaddled loosely in a blanket, back to Karen.

"She has quite a set of lungs, our little Abbie. You did so well. How are you, my love?" Jason leaned down and kissed his wife.

Rachel gazed up at his grinning face. "She does, doesn't she? I'm tired and exhilarated and wonderful, and I can't wait to have her in my arms."

Jason helped her to sit up, fluffing the pillows behind her.

"Your wish is my command." Karen returned with the baby. Rachel held up her arms toward Karen. "Give her to me. Please. I need to hold her."

Karen placed the rosy skinned baby in her mother's arms. "So you're naming her Abbie? That's a lovely name."

"We thought so." Rachel never took her gaze off the baby. "She's named after Jason's mother."

"Oh, how nice. Do you need help with getting her to nurse? Sometimes babies have a difficult time latching on."

"I don't know, I think I can do it."

Rachel put Abbie to her breast and teased the baby with her nipple, rubbing it across her lips, until she opened and took the nub in her mouth and began to suckle.

"Bravo. That the fastest I think I've seen a new mother get her baby to nurse." *The placenta will be easier to deliver now since her womb will clamp down and stop the bleeding.*

Rachel looked up at her and beamed.

"Abbie is a smart girl," crowed Jason.

"I can see that. And I see she has a very proud papa, too. Now I need to deliver the placenta. This will take another few minutes." She pressed down on Rachel's abdomen, moving her hands around until the placenta was out of the birth canal and Karen could pull it out, examining it to make sure it was whole. Thankfully, it was and she wrapped it in a towel to be disposed of. "You'll need to wear your menstrual pad for a few days. If the discharge turns red again, come get me immediately. I have a paper with these instructions that I'll leave on the bureau. Read them so you don't forget." Karen washed her hands and repacked her doctor bag, getting it ready for the next patient.

Jason put his shoulders back and puffed his chest out.

"Yes, I am. A *very* proud papa."

"All right I'll leave now. You can pay me tomorrow when I come back tomorrow and make sure you're not having any problems."

"No, I'll pay you now. What do I owe you?"

"Three dollars will cover it."

Jason handed her a five dollar bill. "Thank you, Karen. I'll walk you down."

"That's all right, I know the way and you need to be here with your wife and daughter. I'm sure someone will take me home."

Rachel looked up from staring at Abbie. "I know Adam would love to take you."

Karen frowned. "I'm not so sure about that, but someone is available, I'm sure."

Jason and Rachel looked at each other with furrowed brows.

"All will be fine. Don't worry," said Karen.

She and Lucy went down to the living room.

"Everyone, you have a new niece and Billy, you have a baby sister. Abbie Talbot. You can all go see her in a half hour or so. Mommy and Daddy need some time alone with her. And I need someone to take me home, if you please."

"I'll take you." Adam stood.

Karen's eyes widened. "That's nice of you."

A smile transformed his face from forbidding to inviting. "My pleasure."

Her cheeks warmed but she kept eye contact. "Thank you."

"Are you ready to go now?"

"Yes, please I'd like to get some sleep. The patients start arriving earlier and earlier every day."

"Here, let me take that."

He reached for her bag and as she gave it to him, their hands touched. Karen looked up to see his eyes had widened again. *He feels it, too. Both times. A connection. Something I've never felt before. My only experience touching ungloved hands is with Douglas and he certainly never gave me this kind of…feeling.*

"Shall we go?"

She nodded drawing in a breath. "Yes." She turned to the people in the room. "Goodnight, all. See you tomorrow."

When they got to the buggy, Adam helped her in again, but this time knowing there was something special between them she was prepared to *feel* the tingle again. But, she didn't. She thought she must have been mistaken when she felt the lightning before. Yes, that was it. She wanted too much for something to be there, something extraordinary.

They were half way down the mountain before she decided to break the silence.

"So, Adam, how would you like to come to dinner next Sunday?"

"I can't. Family things going on."

He sounds angry. Maybe I shouldn't have asked him. "Oh. Family always should come first."

Silence reigned, and she didn't broach the subject of dinner again.

They arrived back at her house just past midnight and she was glad she'd grabbed her shawl before leaving. Adam came around to assist her. This time he lifted her and brought her close to his body as he let her down. She felt his breath on her face and looked up to see him gazing at her with what she was sure was...*hunger*. Well if that was the case...why didn't he just kiss her? No sooner had she processed the thought than he set her away from him.

But she knew what she saw and the sight gave her hope. She would ask him again and rather than Sunday, she'd try for a Saturday dinner.

"Thank you for bringing me home."

He ducked his head. "Sure. Anytime."

Then he departed and she watched the buggy until it was swallowed by the darkness.

The spark between them needed to be explored. Was she brave enough to go after what...no, who...she wanted?

CHAPTER 2

Karen was the most amazing woman Adam'd ever met. A great mother and great doctor, too. She was so much more than just a midwife, treating everything from a cold to gunshot wounds. But she was still a woman, and women were only interested in one thing.

Hadn't Phoebe Eagleton proved that fact? That women were only after money? She'd betrayed him on their wedding day by eloping with his best man and best friend Ralph Jenson. Ralph was rich, almost Croesus rich. Adam hoped they were very happy these last ten years. His brothers were lucky. They found women to love who weren't gold diggers. He should have known something was different with Phoebe when she started wearing her low-cut evening gowns during the day when Ralph was there.

He'd loved Phoebe and that was why he hurt so much from their betrayal. But he'd learned his lesson. He wouldn't fall in love. He wouldn't be that vulnerable ever again.

But Karen seemed different. She wanted to help people and that was all. At least he was pretty sure that was all.

He pulled up to the barn, unharnessed the horse and took him inside to care for him before putting the buggy away.

When he entered the house through the kitchen, he was greeted at the door by a barrage of questions from his sister-in-law, Lucy.

"So what did you and Karen talk about? Will you start courting her?"

"No." Adam closed his eyes and took a deep breath. "She asked me to dinner, but I said no."

"No?" Lucy slapped her forehead and rolled her eyes. "What were you thinking?"

"The invitation was for Sunday. You know that is family day." He frowned at having to explain family time. "We always have dinner all together on Saturday and Sunday."

Lucy put her hands on her hips. "I think you could miss one. Or more. Take control here, Adam. Karen's a wonderful woman and she obviously likes you or she wouldn't have invited you to dinner."

He shoved his hands in his pockets. "I know. I'm not ready for a relationship."

"Since when?" Michael asked as he passed by, headed for the living room. "Phoebe was a long time ago. You have to let that go. Move on, brother. It's been ten years."

Adam raised his arms. *When Michael says ten years, it does sound like a long time.* "I know. I don't need to be lectured to. Not by you or anyone." He stomped up the stairs to his room and slammed the door.

He'd have to apologize for his fit of temper, but his outburst was worth it to see the looks on their faces when normally quiet Adam talked back. What was he so angry about anyway? Hadn't he thought the same things himself?

I would like to get to know Karen better. Maybe I should start courting her. But am I really ready to put Phoebe's betrayal behind me? Karen is so different from Phoebe. I think the time has come to think about marrying. I hadn't thought about getting a readymade family but Larry and Patty seem like good kids.

And Karen would make a wonderful wife. Lucy's right. What was I thinking? I need to take control of the situation and go after who I want. And I want Karen.

Two days later, Adam set out with purpose to talk to Karen. He went by her house, which she'd just moved into. It was now her doctor's office as well and he found it full of people waiting to see her. He looked at his watch. The time was eleven-thirty and it was obvious to him she wouldn't stop to fix a meal.

Smiling, he went back home and prepared lunch for her, which she could eat between patients. He made enough for her children as well. Roast beef sandwiches with butter, sugar cookies and apples. He also took a jug of cold milk and loaded all of the food into his saddle bags.

Back at her house he waited in the living room with the rest of the patients until she came out to get someone else.

"Excuse me, Karen? I have something for you," he said.

Karen gazed at him her eyes wide.

Her luscious pink lips parted.

"Adam. How nice to see you. Follow me to the kitchen where we can talk."

Away from prying eyes, thought Adam.

Once in the kitchen Karen asked, glancing at the saddle bags on his shoulder, "What can I do for you?"

He smiled, walked over and set the saddle bags on the counter by the sink. "Nothing. It's something I can do for you. I know you won't have time to prepare food for lunch so I brought you some. I didn't know if the kids would be here, but there is plenty for them, too."

"Oh, Adam." She sighed, with a smile. "That's so sweet of you. The children are not here, but are with Alice at the dormitory. I have too many patients and the house is much too busy, on Monday's especially, for them to be under foot."

He looked in cupboards and found plates and glasses. "I know you can only have a few bites now, but I'd like to stay."

"And I'd like to have you come to dinner on Saturday."

He shook his head. "I can't on Saturday or Sunday."

She frowned and looked down.

Adam hated to see her sad, so he quickly stated what he'd really come there for. "Family days. But why don't you join us? Bring the kids. They'll love playing with the kittens in the barn and the dogs will pester them something terrible to be petted."

Karen looked at him, tilted her head and bit the inside of her lip. "I don't know...I—"

"You have to take a day off and you need to eat. I'll pick you up about eleven."

She smiled and arched her perfect black brow. "Very sure of yourself aren't you?"

"Yes, ma'am. After all you've invited me to dinner twice now. I figure you must want to get to know me and I want to get to know you as well." *Why did I fight this the other day?*

She pursed her lips and their rosy softness called to him. He had to stop himself from pulling her into his arms and kissing her senseless.

Adam put his hands in his pockets to keep from acting on his urges.

"Since the kids aren't here, would you like to have lunch with me? It looks like there is plenty of food."

His cheeks warmed. "I was hoping you'd ask."

Karen chuckled. "Ah, I think you knew I would, even if the children had been here. They don't eat that much. Six sandwiches are three times as many as we would eat. Let me tell the patients waiting that I'll be back in fifteen minutes that I'm taking a break."

He watched her step out of the kitchen into the living room. A few minutes later she returned.

They sat at the table where Adam set the plates and glasses.

Karen poured them each a glass of the cold milk and placed the rest in the icebox.

"Larry and Patty will love having fresh milk. I only get milk about once a week and it goes fast. Those two both love it."

Adam didn't like that she would have to mete out milk, something he took for granted. "We have two milk cows now. I'll start bringing you some everyday. The kids should have it to grow strong."

Karen's back stiffened and her mouth formed a thin line. "I do the best I can."

Adam waved his hands in front of him and shook his head. "Don't misunderstand. I think you do a fantastic job. You're a great mother. Your kids are polite, funny, and seem to get along with everyone. That's a testament to you as a parent."

She eased back in her chair and relaxed. "Thank you. I appreciate you saying that. Making a living and raising the children has been a struggle since Douglas was killed."

Adam picked up a sandwich. He wanted to get to know her, but deciding what to ask and what not to was difficult in any new relationship.

"How was your husband killed, if you don't mind my asking? If you don't want to talk about it, I understand."

"No. It's fine. He was killed in action just a month after he'd rejoined his Union Army unit. He served as a doctor with the Union Army and their tent had been hit with cannon balls. Not just one but a barrage. Everyone, doctor and patient alike in that tent had been killed."

He placed his hands around the glass of milk. "A doctor. I shouldn't be surprised since you're one, too."

She shook her head. "Not quite. I went to medical school, but didn't graduate. I married Douglas in my senior year and got pregnant right away, so I had to drop out. He didn't want me working anyway, so my expecting was probably a blessing." She clasped her hands in front of her on the table. "Once Larry was born, I didn't want to go to work."

He set his empty plate aside and crossed his arms and leaned forward onto the table. "How did you manage to support yourself with a new baby and no husband for so long? My mother wouldn't have been able to do what you have. She only knew how to be a wife and mother. You on the other hand are all that and more."

She picked up a cookie and broke it in two, handing half to him. "I worked a bit as a midwife. And we had some savings. But I had to sell the house and then come here as a mail-order bride before that money was gone and my opportunity to achieve my dream had passed."

He leaned forward until he was at her eye level. "And what is your dream, Karen? What would you like most in the world?" *He hadn't considered that women had dreams of their own. Had his mother had dreams of what to do with her life? Or was raising her children her only desire in life?*

She smiled and looked down, then back up.

It was like she was deciding how much of her dream she would trust him with.

Finally, she gazed steadily at him. "What I really want is to open a clinic, with a real doctor and maybe another midwife." She took a bite of her sandwich.

"Why don't you?"

She held up one finger and swallowed, then sipped her milk to wash the sandwich down. "Money. All the banks in Olympia and Tacoma have turned me down for a loan to build it, because I'm a woman with no husband."

He'd never heard of a woman applying for a loan on her own. She knew he was wealthy, yet she hadn't asked him for money. "That would make it difficult. Where would you build this clinic? Do you have the land for the building?"

"Well, that's another problem in itself."

He surprised himself by saying, "Maybe I can help."

She raised her head until her gaze met his. "You want to help me? But you don't know me."

"Well." He ran a hand behind his neck. "That's another reason I came to see you today. I'd like to get to know you and to start courting you, if you would be amenable to that situation."

He watched her eyes widen and a beautiful pink color traveled up her neck to her cheeks.

She focused on her hands but nodded. "I am amenable to have you court me." Then she looked up and held his gaze with her own. "Are you sure you want an instant family? Larry and Patty are good children, but they might be resentful at not having me all to themselves."

Adam sat back in his chair. "I'm certain I can win them over. I generally get along well with children." *Billy used to come to me when he was upset with his father and the kids in town know I'm good for a stick of candy. Maybe that's why they like me.*

She smiled. "Good. I'm glad. Would you like to come to dinner tomorrow night? We can talk more."

"Yes." He smiled. "I'd like that very much. Can I bring anything?"

"No. I'm only preparing an easy meal. We generally eat simply. I'm not a great cook."

He put his forearms on the table and grinned. "That's all right, because I am."

"Maybe you should come in time to prepare dinner as well," she said with a laugh.

"Well, I could—"

Karen reached over and placed a hand on his arm. "Adam, I'm kidding. I will fix dinner. Be here at six. I should be done with my patients before then."

"I'll be here, but you should post your hours. I understand that people will come any time if you don't."

I know how to run my business, but I realize he's simply trying to help. "I intend to do just that, but I just haven't gotten around to it."

"I'll make you one. I want to have time with you so we can get to know each other. That won't happen if you don't make office hours."

Karen sighed and sagged in her chair. "You're right and I need to spend more time with my children as well. I've been working so much I begin to wonder if they know I'm still their mother instead of Alice, the girl who watches them for me."

"Raising two children and working in a profession such as yours must be difficult."

She nodded. "It is but I do what I have to for my kids. They are the most important people in my life."

That is as it should be but can I accept being second?

Karen felt his warm hand in hers and was comforted, but would rather have his strong arms around her. She wanted to burrow into his body so she'd always feel this way. She had a hope of not being alone. But what if he couldn't accept parenting two youngsters? Her children were everything to her. All that she did was for them. Building a clinic was for them, so she'd spend more time with them.

After a few moments, and much too soon, she pulled back her hand.

"What if you get to know me and don't like what you find?"

Adam slowly shook his head. "I can assure you that won't happen. I already admire you and I can't imagine that changing."

"I can't, either, but I think we should take this slow. Start with dinner tomorrow and then go forward from there." She picked up their dishes and took them to the sink. "For now though, I must return to my patients."

"I understand. I'll let myself out the kitchen door."

"Thank you. See you tomorrow night."

"Six o'clock on the button. You can set your watch by me." He picked up the saddle bags off the counter and threw them over his shoulder.

She laughed. "Go now before I do something I shouldn't." *And kiss you the way I want to.*

"I'm going."

Karen watched him leave and then went back to her patients, though she didn't think she could concentrate.

Shaking her head she smoothed her skirt and went into the living room which was jammed with people...as it would be every day.

Did Adam really want to court her? Would he come or would some family business get in the way?

CHAPTER 3

Adam came home early from work. He'd spent the day interviewing men who wanted a position as a lumberjack and women who were applying to be the camp cook. He dressed with care for his dinner with Karen and her children. Wearing his best white shirt, black wool jacket and pants, he thought he would make a reasonably good impression. He didn't want to go empty handed so he asked Rachel to bake a pie made from the tinned cherries in the pantry.

When she heard he wanted to take it to Karen's for dinner, she couldn't wait to bake the dessert.

He took the buggy because he couldn't carry the pie on a horse. Adam wanted tonight to be special and smelling like an animal would not endear him to Karen, in his estimation.

Arriving at Karen's, he checked his watch. Five fifty-nine. By the time he walked up to the door, it would be six o'clock on the nose.

He knocked and the door was answered by Karen's six year old son,

"Hi, mister. Who are you?"

"I'm Adam. And you must be Larry. I've heard stories about you."

Wide-eyed, the boy looked up at him. "You have?"

"Yes. Your mama is very proud of you."

Larry grinned from ear to ear.

"Mama, Adam's here," he yelled as he ran for the door to the kitchen.

A minute later, Karen emerged looking beautiful in a simple pink blouse and gray skirt. He smiled. Actually, she looked elegant.

She lifted her hand to him.

He grasped it, brought it to his lips and kissed the top, delighted to see her blush.

"Come in please. Dinner is about ready. The children are eating right now and should be finished by the time our meal is complete."

"I assumed they would be eating with us, but I don't mind having your complete attention. I didn't come empty handed." He gave her the pie. "Rachel made it. I don't bake very well."

"Oh, thank you. The pie is very thoughtful. What kind is it?"

"It's cherry and you're welcome. Will the children want some?"

"Most definitely. We'll all have dessert together. But the children can play while we eat. That will give us an opportunity to talk. Follow me, please."

She turned and returned to the kitchen. Both children were at the table and eating with gusto for such little people. He was surprised thinking from Karen's earlier statement about the sandwiches being more than they could eat that they were light eaters.

Patty was about three years old and the spitting image of her mother except her hair was brown not quite black like Karen's.

Larry on the other hand must have resembled his father for his hair was as light as his mother and sister's was dark.

Karen stood next to Adam at the end of the table. "Children. This is Adam Talbot. He is here to have dinner with me. When you finish your meals, you will go into the living room and play quietly until bedtime. All right?"

"Why do we have to go?" Larry whined.

"Yeah, no want to go," pouted Patty her arms crossed over her chest.

"You will do as I say or you will go to bed right now. Am I understood?"

Both children hung their heads. "Yes, Mama," said Larry.

"Yes, Mama," repeated Patty.

Adam didn't want to be thought of as the bad guy, stealing time with their mama.

"Karen, they'll be back before bed, right?"

She nodded and smiled. "Adam brought us pie for dessert. If you're good, you'll come back in here to have a piece with us before bed. All right?"

"Yay!" hollered Larry.

Patty bounced up and down in her chair. "Pie. Pie. Pie."

"Calm down and eat," laughed Karen.

When the kids finished eating they took their plates to the sink. Larry helped Patty with hers as the little girl was too small to reach the counter. Then they ran to the living room.

Karen turned to Adam. "Please sit." She pointed at the chair that was across from where Larry had sat.

He sat where she indicated. "You really do have very good children. When Billy was their ages, he was so spoiled. I'm afraid all of us gave him whatever he wanted. We were terrible fathers, except for Jason. He realized that Billy needed rules and discipline in order to grow into a good man."

"Thank you. I am proud of my children. They mind very well, usually, but they're excited to have company. As am I."

Karen dished up their plates from the pots on the stove and the plate in the warming oven. She'd prepared fried steak, mashed potatoes, gravy, green beans and, to his surprise, fresh bread.

"When did you find time to bake bread?"

She waved away the question. "I start it in the morning, let it rise and punch it down a couple of times between patients and then bake it in the afternoon. I just have to make sure I don't put it in the oven and then take a patient that will need more time than the fifty minute baking time."

"Well, you do it very well." He buttered a piece of the fluffy bread. "This is great. I'm usually not around for the first slice of bread. We all like the heels, especially when it's hot, right from the oven. When you butter it, the slice ends up with butter pooled in it. So good. As a matter of fact the whole meal looks fantastic."

"Good. Let's eat."

They were silent for a few minutes while they started their meals.

"So, Adam. What is your position with Talbot Lumber?"

"What don't I do would be a better question. I do everything except the books. Jason is the one who does those. The rest of us manage work crews and even work as lumberjacks ourselves. I've been the camp cook more times than I can remember. The task always seems to fall to me if the regular cook is sick or quits before I can hire a new one. Today I spent the day interviewing for lumberjack and the camp cook."

"Does all your lumber go through Alfred Pope's mill before going on the market?"

"How do you know so much about the lumber business?"

"I made it a point to understand your business as much as possible, when I arrived. I like to know what type of people I'll be dealing with."

Adam nodded. "That's a good practice. Back to your question, most of the wood does go through the mill to make lumber, but we do get orders for raw timber as well. The customer will want a certain size to use as ship masts, for instance. Railroads need them for the ties for the tracks and they have to be cut to a specific size."

"The operation sounds interesting."

Adam set down his fork between bites. "You just say that because you want to make a good impression. I've got news for you. You already have. What you do is not just interesting but amazing. You heal people and save their lives. *That* is interesting."

Karen ducked her chin, but she smiled. "That's very kind of you to say."

He crossed his heart. "I only speak the truth. The work you do must be very fulfilling. As a midwife, have you lost a baby or a mother? Do women often bleed to death, like Jason's first wife, Cassie?"

A cloud seemed to shadow her face. "I've never lost a mother, but I lost a baby once. Very nearly lost his mother, too. He was breech you see, and I had a particularly bad time getting him turned so he could be born. When I did and he finally joined us, I discovered the umbilical cord wrapped around his neck. The baby was born dead. His mother was inconsolable."

Adam's gut clenched. He reached over and covered her hand with his. "I'm so sorry. That must have been terrible."

"It was. I try not to think about it, but every time I deliver a new baby, I can't help it. The memory comes unbidden to me, even in all the chaos that comes with birthing. I try to push it back into the recesses of my mind, but sometimes only the joy on the new parent's faces makes it leave my consciousness."

"I'm glad that your work can bring you so much joy. Not many people can say that what they do for a living is more than tolerable, much less joyous."

She smiled and retrieved her hand. "How can bringing a new life into the world be anything but a blissful occasion?"

He removed his hand to the side of his empty plate.

"Dinner has been great. I want to do it again soon. Perhaps with the children. I do want them to get to know me."

"I know and I said they would have dinner with us when I asked you, but I decided I wanted us to talk alone. You can start now." Karen pushed back her chair and stood. "Shall we have the pie with coffee?"

He smiled. "I almost forgot. I'd love that. Should I get the kids while you cut us each a slice? If I cut it, I'll give the little ones too much."

"That would be wonderful."

She started clearing the dinner dishes.

He touched her hand as she reached for his plate. "Here. Let me do that."

"Adam, you'll spoil me."

He stood close to her, lifted his hand and cupped her face. "You deserve to be spoiled."

Her blue-eyed gaze met his and he watched her blush. He liked to make her color rise. She looked like a beautiful pink rose.

She leaned into his hand and closed her eyes.

Her response to his touch was good. Very good. He effected her in the way he wanted. He pleased her and that pleased him.

Leaning away from his touch, she composed herself back to the no nonsense mother and midwife. "You get the children and I'll cut the pie. Don't let them talk you into playing with them. They need to eat their dessert and go to bed."

"All right. We'll be right back."

Karen couldn't believe she'd just done that. Leaned into his hand like a schoolgirl with her first crush. Just the thought brought heat to her cheeks. She pulled plates out of the cupboard and cut the pie, giving Adam a large slice, the children small ones and her somewhere in the middle. Just like The Three Bears story. She chuckled under her breath.

She took the pie to the table and then poured milk for the children and coffee for her and Adam. By the time she had dessert ready, Adam and the kids were coming through the doorway from the living room.

She looked around her little abode. What did Adam see when he looked at her kitchen? An extension of her or just the light wood cabinets, drawers and plain counter top? The white curtains with little pink fleur-de-lis' or a woman's whimsy?

"Come everyone take your seats and let's eat this delicious pie Adam brought us."

"Yay! Pie!" yelled Larry, running to the table.

"Yay!" echoed Patty, hot on his heels.

"Should I holler 'yay', too?" Adam grinned.

"If you want. The more the merrier," said Karen. The children climbed into their chairs and started eating as fast as they could, as if they were afraid the delectable offering would disappear. Unfortunately, the kids weren't used to having dessert and that made her sad. Was she really a good mother?

Adam smiled.

Karen felt relieved that he could actually be entertained by her babies. They were everything to her, and if he had been upset at their lack of manners when given a treat, she'd know the relationship would not work. Any man, especially this man, needed to get along with her children.

A knock sounded on the front door.

Adam checked his watch, then frowned. "Patients at this hour? I really must get you a sign."

"Excuse me. I must go. Would you keep an eye on the kids for me?"

"Of course."

Karen walked through the living room to the front door.

"May I help you," she said to the woman standing there. Then she recognized who it was. "Mrs. Jacobsen? What are you doing here? In Seattle?"

The woman, a short woman with mousy brown hair, looked the worse for wear. Her coat was tattered. The green dress which showed under the open coat was not in much better shape.

She smiled. "I came to warn you, though why I don't know. I'll have my revenge on you, Karen Martell. You stole my baby from me."

Karen stiffened her back and slowly shook her head. *This couldn't be real. How was she here? How can I convince her nothing I did would have made a difference?* "Mrs. Jacobsen. Anna. Your baby dead when he was born. I did everything I could to save your baby. I wish above all else that the circumstance had not happened. The cord was around his neck and being in the breech position, he couldn't get the oxygen he needed. I'm so sorry."

"Not yet you're not. But you will be."

The woman turned and ran down the steps into the dark, her maniacal cackle fading into the night.

Karen shut the door and leaned against it waiting for her heart to stop racing before she joined the others in the kitchen.

How did she find me? Are my children in danger? Am I? What does she want from me?

CHAPTER 4

Adam looked up and smiled as Karen re-entered the kitchen. His smile faded and he jumped out of his seat rushing to her.

"What happened? You're pale as a sheet?"

"Nothing. Not now." She looked over at her children. The pie was finished and they were drinking the milk like it was ambrosia they'd never get again. "All right. Later."

"Children." Karen clapped her hands twice. "Time for bed now. Go get in your pajamas."

Larry looked up, ready to challenge her.

Adam narrowed his eyes and shook his head.

The child stood. "I have to go potty."

"All right." Karen looked at Adam. "We'll be right back. Patty, you come, too."

"Otay." She skipped to the door.

They returned in about five minutes and Adam stood from the table.

"Are you ready for bed now?" asked Karen.

"Uh huh. 'Night, Mama."

He looked up and pursed his lips for a kiss.

"Goodnight, my little love."

Patty was right behind.

"'Night."

Karen picked up the toddler and cuddled her.

"Goodnight, my littlest love."

She set the child down and the two children left the room.

Adam fixed his gaze on Karen. "Are you all right, now? Can we talk?"

She nodded. "After I put them down. Give me a few minutes to tell them a story and get them to sleep. Thank you for staying. I could use a friend."

"Anytime you need me, I'll be here."

Adam walked to the stove and filled his coffee cup. The way Karen looked, it might be a long night and he would be here for as long as she needed him.

He waited for about fifteen minutes before she returned; wondering all the while what could have scared her so.

When she entered the kitchen, she wasn't as pale and she had something in her hand.

She set the small box on the counter and then picked up her cup. "I think I'll join you in that coffee." She walked to the stove and filled the cup.

He waited until she was seated and had a sip of the hot brew.

"Ready to tell me what happened when you answered the door?" He spoke softly so as not to wake the children.

She nodded. "Remember the story I told you about the baby I lost?"

"I do. Breech birth and the cord around his neck."

"Correct. Well, his mother was at the door. She threatened me. She said I'd be sorry for taking her baby from her. What does she mean?"

"I don't know." Concern filled him but he didn't let it show. "I think you should have someone with you at all times."

She shook her head. "That's a nice thought, but I still have patients to see."

"I'm thinking about a man who would be in your waiting room all day and someone else who would watch the house at night." He reached over and covered her hand with his. "I'll be with you as often as I can."

Karen sighed. "I can't pay someone to watch me. I don't have that kind of money."

"You don't have to. I have two men in mind. They were sheriffs in Arizona Territory and came here to make their fortunes as lumberjacks. I think they'll be happy for the easier duty." He leaned forward and whispered. "Lumberjacking is hard work. I don't care who you are."

Her eyes widened and she shook her head. "I can't let you do that. You barely know me."

He squeezed her hand lightly. "I intend for us to get to know each other much better. I believe we've agreed that I may court you with the result being marriage. I would do this if you were my wife. Let me do it now."

Tears formed in her beautiful eyes that were such a deep blue they reminded him of the ocean on the voyage here.

"I don't know what to say."

"Yes. Just say yes."

She smiled. "All right. If those men are agreeable, then so am I. But don't force them. Since they left their previous employment, perhaps they'd rather not go back to acting like lawmen."

He relinquished her hand, sure he'd held it too long, but it felt so right in his. "I know they will be quite amenable to the position. They'll get the same wage and won't have to climb up fifty feet in a tree. What our men do is very dangerous, and I think Quinn and Abe will like a break from it. I know I would. I used to do the lumberjack work. All of the Talbots did, even Michael who chose to ranch instead."

"You don't climb trees now that you employ so many men. What is it? More than one hundred I would guess."

He nodded. "You'd be right. One hundred and six men to be exact. As to what I do, I manage the men. Which is why I know how many we have. We're always hiring, though. The crews turn over rather fast when the men find out just how hard the work is."

"I can imagine."

He was relieved that her posture had relaxed and color returned to her face. He placed his hands around his coffee cup and tilted his head. "Do you feel better now? Safer?"

"I do." She touched his arm. "Thank you, Adam. I don't know how I'll ever repay you. Do you think we should tell the sheriff? I think Brand should be made aware that this woman is somewhat unhinged. To think she followed me all the way here. And from the looks of her, it took every bit of money she could scrape together just to make the trip."

He nodded. *I'll use every resource I have to keep Karen safe.* "We do need to inform him. He can keep an eye out for her."

She furrowed her eyebrows. "I wonder where she's sleeping. I doubt she's at the Seattle Inn. That would take money and be too obvious considering the threat she made."

"You're right. A couple of flop houses are just outside of town. She might be in one of those. From what you've said, I can't picture her making a camp outside under the stars."

"I can't either."

Adam pointed at the counter. "What's the little box for?"

Karen glanced the way he pointed. "It's my grandmother's music box. I usually let it play and the music puts the children to sleep. It stopped working a few days ago so, when I get time, I'll see if I can fix it."

"Will you be all right tonight? Do you want me to stay? I can sleep on your sofa."

"That's okay. I'm fine. I just won't answer the door." She smiled. "Now is past office hours anyway."

He nodded and grinned. "It is at that."

She set down the coffee cup and stood. "Well, I guess I should get myself to bed. Thank you, Adam, for coming to dinner and being here to help me. When should I expect the first man to arrive?"

He stood and took her hand in both of his. "First, I'm glad I was here, too. Just get me a message whenever you need me. I'll drop everything to be here. Second, I'll have Quinn take the first shift. He'll be here at seven o'clock if that meets with your approval."

She didn't remove her hand from his. "That would be perfect. But if he wants to be here for breakfast have him come a half an hour earlier."

"I'm sure he would appreciate that." He glanced down at their hands and squeezed hers lightly. "I'll send him at six-thirty."

"Great." Slowly she removed her hand from his and put it by her side. "I'll show you out."

"I'll follow you." *I'm happy I could relieve her worries.*

When she opened the door, he leaned down and gave her a chaste kiss on the cheek. "Don't worry. All will be well."

"I'm much less worried now."

"Good. See you tomorrow."

"Goodnight."

"Sleep well."

He turned and walked to the buggy.

I wonder if I'm giving her enough protection. Should I have two men outside, even during the day?

At precisely six-thirty in the morning, Karen answered the door. The children were already up and dressed. She'd just started dishing up their breakfasts when the knock sounded.

A tall, good-looking man, with long blond, wavy hair, and plaid flannel shirt, stood on the porch.

"Mrs. Martell?"

"I'm Karen Martell. You must be Quinn. Please come in." She waved an arm taking in the room and held the door wide. "You're right on time for breakfast. I hope scrambled eggs, bacon and biscuits are to your liking."

He removed his hat and hung it on one of the pegs near the door. "Oh, yes ma'am. All are my favorites. As a matter of fact, any food is my favorite." He chuckled at his jest.

Karen pointed at the table where her children sat eating. "Take a seat Mr. Quinn."

"It's Quinn, ma'am, just Quinn."

Larry looked up from his seat at the table, mouth full of eggs. "Who are you?"

Quinn walked over to her son and extended his hand. "I'm Quinn. Who are you?"

"Don't talk with your mouth full," Karen admonished her son.

He swallowed. "I'm Larry. I'm six." He pointed at Quinn's holster. "Is that a real gun?"

Quinn smiled. "It is. You're awfully young to be the man of the house, but I think you must be doing a fine job."

Her boy puffed out his chest and grinned. "I am."

She lifted an eyebrow and turned to Quinn. "You must call me Karen. Ma'am makes me sound like I'm a hundred years old."

He chuckled. "You're anything but old."

She smiled. "Thank you. Your observation makes me feel better." She dished up a heaping plate of food for the man and much smaller portions for herself.

He waved his arm, taking in the room. "You're house is right nice, ma'am...er Karen."

"I'm glad you like it. So where do you call home, Quinn?"

"I reckon that'd be Texas. That's where I was born, but I never thought about staying there. As soon as I was old enough to fend for myself, I left and haven't ever looked back." He picked up his fork and scooped up some eggs. "You came as one of the brides from back east, right?"

What is his opinion of the brides, me included? "That's correct."

"I figure moving all the way across the country takes a lot of guts to begin with and you with kids even. I don't know many women and no men who would do that in your situation."

"I had no choice. I could become a mail-order bride or live in the streets."

He grinned.

His smile was endearing, showing a crooked front tooth which made him look like a kid.

"There you see. You did have a choice. You just made the best one for you."

Karen couldn't help but smile. "I guess you're right. Care for more coffee?"

"Mama," said Larry. "May we be excused?"

"You may, and thank you for asking."

The child beamed and he and his sister ran to the living room to play.

Karen turned back to Quinn. "I understand that you will be in the living room today. It serves as my waiting room. Did you bring something to read? Have you been given a description of the woman?"

"Yes. Adam filled me in. And I brought a book I just got." He pulled a book from his inside vest pocket. "*Moby Dick* by Hermann Melville. I'm told it's a good book about a big, white whale. We'll see. I've never seen a white whale, so it doesn't sound too believable to me."

Karen stood and picked up the children's dishes. "I've read the book and it is very good. You'll enjoy it."

As she reached for Quinn's plate, he stood. "Let me help you with that."

She shook her head. "No, thank you. You go on and get settled. After I finish the dishes, I'll bring you a cup of coffee and open the door for the first patients to start filing in. You can keep an eye on the kids for me." *His presence eases my mind about keeping them in line.*

"That I can do."

He turned and headed for the living room.

Karen finished cleaning the kitchen and was headed to the examination room.

A knock sounded at the kitchen door. Her heart beat a rapid tattoo.

A second pounding knock came and she decided to face what or who was on the other side.

Quinn entered the kitchen. "Karen, don't open that door. Let me." He pulled his pistol from his holster and walked to the door.

He opened it and holstered his gun.

Apparently, no one was there. He started to shut the door and frowned, pulling a piece of paper off the door.

Her stomach roiled as Karen accepted the note from his outstretched hand. Quinn closed and locked the door behind him before following her to the table where she slumped into a chair. With shaking hands she unfolded the paper.

I'll get what's due to me and you'll suffer just like me.

Her body quaked. She needed Adam. Needed someone to lean on. But she didn't want him to think she'd come running to him every time something scared her. She wasn't that kind of woman.

But this was too much. The woman struck fear in Karen like she'd never felt before. She knew Anna was determined, she'd come all the way to Seattle to make Karen hurt like she had, but Karen wasn't sure what that meant.

CHAPTER 5

Ethan Steward waited for his luggage to be brought up from his cabin on the *Bonnie Blue.* He'd just arrived from San Francisco. He'd been there for three months and tired of the gambling, drinking and carousing. Visiting his Talbot cousins seemed like just the thing to take his mind off the losses he'd suffered at the gaming tables. The money wasn't enough to break him. Barely equaled the interest on his bank accounts for one year, but that was too much. He wasn't normally one for frittering away money on activities like gambling. He gambled enough every day with his investments. But he was on vacation and wanted to taste the vices of San Francisco.

He hoped visiting his cousins would provide a distraction. Perhaps he'd even try his hand at lumberjacking. No, probably not. That was hard work and Ethan had never done any real physical labor in his life. No need to start now.

The captain of the Bonnie Blue, Clancy Adams, had pointed the way to the Talbot home and Ethan now trekked up that road, if you could call it a road, to his cousin Jason's house.

He was surprised that the weather was much warmer here than in San Francisco, yet the overcast sky made it cool enough he wasn't sweating as he walked up the hill.

The town of Seattle was not what he was expecting. The buildings were rustic, most made from logs, probably from his cousin's lumber. The four large white clapboard buildings he passed seemed out of place with the rest of the town. He'd have to ask about that.

And he passed many more young women than he expected to see. He thought the town was mostly lumberjacks, but he was wrong.

A tall, slender woman with brown hair, dressed in pants and a younger woman with red hair passed him by, heading down to Seattle. She must be coming from Jason's.

"Hello," said the woman as she passed.

Ethan doffed his hat. "Hello, ladies."

The women giggled but kept on walking.

Interesting thought Ethan as he watched them walk away. Very interesting. He continued on to Jason's.

He found the three-story log home with no trouble and climbed the stairs to the wide front porch. Out of breath, he waited until he was more under control. Finally, he took a deep breath and released it, put a smile on his face and knocked.

A pretty blonde woman answered the door holding a tiny baby.

"May I help you?"

Ethan quickly doffed his bowler hat.

"Yes, ma'am. I'm Ethan Steward, and I'm looking for my cousin Jason Talbot. I was told he lives here."

She smiled.

And looked absolutely radiant, thought Ethan.

"Please come inside. I'm Rachel, Jason's wife and this is Abbie, our daughter. She's a week old today. Follow me to Jason's office. He's working right now, but I'm sure he'll be thrilled to see you."

He followed her to a room just off the kitchen. A strange place to locate an office, he thought.

Rachel knocked once and opened the door.

Jason didn't look up. "Hello, my loves. Be right with you."

Rachel giggled. "Jason. You have a visitor... besides me and Abbie."

Jason turned, a questioning look on his face which transformed to a smile. He stood and walked to Ethan. "My gosh, Ethan, you've grown up. What are you now? Twenty-five or six?" He gave the young man a bear hug. "Let's go to the kitchen, and I'll pour us some coffee. Rachel, this is my cousin, Ethan Steward. Come. Come."

Rachel turned and led the way.

The kitchen was Spartan compared to his home in New Bedford. Lots of cupboards, a huge four door ice box, a six burner stove and a double sink with a pump on the side. A door near the stove he thought must be the pantry. Next to the office was a door leading outside, he saw trees through the window.

Ethan sat at the table. Rachel handed Jason his daughter. "Why don't you see if you can put her to sleep? She just won't do it for me. I think she's afraid she'll miss something." She chuckled and got them each a cup of hot coffee from the pot on the stove.

"So, what are you doing in Seattle? Looking to become a lumberjack? Are you broke?" Jason stood and rocked Abbie. She gurgled and milk dribbled from the side of her mouth. Jason wiped her lips and put her up on his shoulder and patted her back.

"No, to all of those questions. I simply got tired of San Francisco and decided I'd come visit my Talbot cousins."

Jason reached over and clapped him on the back. "Glad to have you here. Tell us what's happening back in New Bedford."

"I'm not sure. I haven't been home in about a year."

Soon Abbie let it be known that she was tired of not being the center of attention.

Jason sniffed the air.

If Ethan's nose wasn't wrong it was time for a diaper change.

Jason handed Abbie to her mother.

"If you gentlemen will excuse me, I need to take care of our little tyrant here. Please continue without me."

Rachel gave Jason a kiss, then left.

"You have a beautiful family, cousin. Where did you find her?"

"It's a long story but to make it short, we brought one hundred women from Massachusetts as brides for the men here. Rachel and Drew's wife Lucy, who'll you'll meet later, were two of those brides."

Ethan leaned back and put his hands in his vest pockets. "And you two had your choice and picked the best. You sly dogs. Rachel is spectacular, and I would bet Lucy is, too."

Jason shook his head. "None of the women were supposed to marry us. We just happened to fall in love."

"Well, congratulations."

Jason accepted Ethan's hand but lifted his brow. Ethan thought maybe he'd given himself away. He intended to find one or more of the brides who were up for a good time, not marriage. Surely, with his good looks, and deep pockets, he wouldn't have a hard time. Maybe a widow. They always want sex now that the husband is dead. Yes, he would find a widow…or two.

Jason didn't like the way Ethan referred to the brides. Something snide about his attitude bothered him. He also knew Ethan thought himself irresistible, not only because of his good looks, but also because of his money.

He'd have to tell Adam to keep an eye on their cousin. As the only single brother, he could do and go wherever Ethan did. Gabe and Drew would be warned as well.

Ethan may be their cousin, but family blood wasn't more important than the brides' reputations.

Adam hurried through his chores. He wanted to get to Karen's as soon as possible and make sure all was well with her and that Quinn was in place.

Walking into the waiting room, he saw Quinn.

He immediately stood and came over. "Can I talk to you outside?"

"Sure."

They walked out and Quinn led him to the far side of the porch.

"Karen received a note this morning, and it has her pretty shook up. She wouldn't tell me the contents of the missive. I think you'd better talk to her."

Anger filled Adam. Karen shouldn't have to be afraid in her own home. He grasped Quinn by the shoulder and put out his hand.

The younger man shook it.

"Thanks for letting me know. I'll talk to her as soon as she's done with her current patient."

Quinn nodded and walked back inside, leaving Adam on the porch.

Adam would have to set men to search for the Jacobsen woman. She had to be found. This terrorism of Karen had to stop.

Taking a deep breath, he walked into the house. Karen had just finished with a patient and was about to take the next one when he jutted his chin in her direction.

She came over to him.

"Will you join me in the kitchen, please?"

"Certainly."

They were keeping their interactions formal. First, Adam didn't want anyone to be interested in what was happening with their doctor. Second, he wasn't ready for the world to know he was courting Karen, unless them knowing they were courting is what she wanted.

When they reached the kitchen, she turned, and he saw the glistening in her eyes.

She pulled a piece of paper from her pocket and handed it to him.

"This note is what she left this morning."

He read the paper and swore, then took a deep breath. "I honestly don't know what to make of it. I'm getting more men to station here. One outside and one inside. She won't be able to get near you or the house again without being seen. At least, that is my hope. Having both men here should protect you, and I'll get together a sort of posse to look for her and find where she's hiding. Not too many places that I can think of would be open to a single woman with no money. We'll find her."

Tears trickled down her cheek.

The sight broke Adam's heart. He opened his arms wide. "Come here."

She shook her head. "I shouldn't need to lean on you."

"Karen." He tilted his head.

She sniffled and rushed into his embrace. "I'm sorry. Sorry to be so needy. I'm not normally so weak."

Her scent wafted up to him. Violets. Unique. "Needing to lean on someone once in a while is not weak. It's human. We all need someone, sometimes."

She looked up at him. "Even you?"

He smiled, hugging her close, her warm body fit his like a glove. He nodded. "Even me."

Standing there for a minute they didn't speak. They just held each other.

Then the moment was broken and she backed away. Swiping her eyes with her palms, she took a deep breath and stiffened her spine.

Adam saw the change in her. She was now determined to beat the woman at whatever game she played.

"I'm fine now. Thank you."

Adam placed his hands in his pants pockets. "Anytime. Quinn is here, your children are safe with the brides and I'm leaving to get together my posse. I'll find her. I promise."

"All right. I'll concentrate on my patients and finding the funding for my clinic."

He struggled with his demons, thinking all women were interested in was money, but Karen he thought was different. She never asked him for money, was thrifty with her own and worked hard to support her children. Pushing his suspicions to the back of his mind, he broached the subject of money. "Speaking of that, have you thought about asking Jason for the money? You'll be buying the lumber from Talbots and he might consider that funding the clinic will be good for the community as well."

Her eyes lit up. "Do you really think he might? I never thought of asking a private business like his before. Can you make an appointment for me? Please?"

"Certainly." He opened his hands, palms up. "You should know that I don't have any influence on him when it comes to finances for the company, so I can't sway his decision."

Karen smiled, walked to him and gave him a hug. "I won't need your help when Jason understands how good the clinic will be for Seattle. He'll agree. I know he will."

He held her and gently rubbed her back. "I think he will, too. Why don't you ask him when you come up next Saturday for family dinner?"

She stepped away and shook her head. "I'd rather keep it professional. The children and I will be there on Saturday, as planned."

"They'll have fun watching the new baby. I do."

"I think they need a little more activity on the part of the baby before they would find watching her entertaining. Abbie is just too young."

He ran a hand through his hair and suddenly realized he didn't know much about what entertains children. "They can play with Billy. He's always been good with the younger kids, since he's always been the oldest child around."

"All right. And then I'll plan on setting an appointment for Monday, to talk to Jason about the loan."

"As you wish. I won't mention it until you do."

"Thank you. That is what I want."

"Although, if we marry, then it would be family funding family and a much easier sell."

She shook her head and her mouth turned down. "I don't want anyone to think I married you for your money. That's definitely not the reason I'd marry you, *if* I marry you. We've agreed to court, with the intent of marriage, but either one of us could change our mind."

Adam frowned. "I don't intend to change my mind."

"I don't either," she admitted. "But, it's possible."

He nodded. "I suppose that's true. Regardless, I'd like to announce at dinner on Saturday that we're courting, if that meets with your approval."

She tilted her head, "Of course. I'd like for your family to know."

He took her hands in his and kissed the top of each one. "You know, courting has been uncharted water for both of us for a long time. But we're in this together and we'll make it." He squeezed her hands just a little. "Right?"

She nodded and smiled. "Right. I should get back to my patients."

"I need to speak to Quinn again."

He followed her out into the living room, filled with patients waiting to see her. Adam was surprised to see a man leaning on the jam of the open door with his arms crossed over his chest and smiling...at Karen. He was even more surprised to realize the man was his cousin.

Adam walked over and held out his hand. "Ethan? I hardly recognize you. You've grown up."

Ethan turned his gaze toward Adam. He stood straight and uncrossed his arms and shook Adam's hand. "We've all changed in the last ten years. Tell me." He jutted his chin toward Karen. "Who is the lovely lady...*doctor*?"

All of Adams senses went on alert. He straightened his back and his hands fisted at his sides. "Why? Are you ill?"

Ethan shook his head and smiled. "Not at all. I think she's beautiful, and I would like to make her acquaintance." He shrugged. "That's all."

Adam thought his smile looked predatory, like a wolf looking at a newborn lamb. He narrowed his eyes. "She is to be my fiancée. She's just agreed to my courting her. Karen is no longer free."

"Ah, I see. But Jason didn't bring it up so he must not know. You haven't announced it yet, have you?" Ethan kept his gaze on Karen. "Until you do, she might be interested in having dinner with me."

"Ethan, don't start out this visit making an enemy of me. Besides she has two children. You wouldn't be interested in a woman with children."

Ethan ducked his head and cocked a brow. "Come on, cousin, I'm not talking marriage here, just a little fun."

Adam tried to control himself. He really did, but his fist seemed to have a mind of its own and hit Ethan in the jaw, knocking him flat on the floor.

"You go near her, and you'll get more of that."

"Adam! What are you doing? Let me help you, young man." She glared at Adam. "I don't know what's gotten into him."

"Don't worry yourself, dear lady." He stood, rubbed his jaw and then wiggled it. "This is just a family dispute. Adam is my cousin." He took her hand and kissed the top. "Would you heal my wound by having dinner with me tonight?"

Karen cocked an eyebrow and smiled. "No, thank you. I am otherwise involved."

She finally withdrew her hand from Ethan's; as Adam was about to bodily remove him from the room.

"Come on. Adam won't mind, will you cousin?"

"I mind very much," he growled.

Karen glanced at Adam and smiled. "Regardless of whether Adam cares or not, you're much too young for me to have dinner with you. People would say unkind things about both of us."

"I don't care what people say."

"Keep your voice down," she reprimanded.

Ethan was persistent. Adam would give him that. Although he would still pound him into the dirt, cousin or not. Karen seemed to be getting tired of the spectacle they were making. All of her patients were paying way too much attention to the three of them.

"Gentlemen. You must leave." Her voice was strained as she whispered as loud as she could, still trying to keep the conversation private. "I have work to do and patients to take care of." She turned to Adam. "I'll see you tonight."

Adam's chest puffed out. He couldn't help it. She clearly chose him in front of everyone and rebuffed his cousin. He'd been right about her. She wasn't like Phoebe. At least so far.

CHAPTER 6

When Saturday came Karen dressed in her nicest day dress of pink seersucker with a round neckline and sleeves that puffed on the upper arm with long cuffs. The garment made her skin appear slightly rosy, instead of just pale, against her black hair. She decided to save her Sunday clothes, a maroon dress with sweetheart neckline and matching jacket and hat, for meeting with Jason on Monday. She made sure her children were presentable and not in their play clothes.

Adam came to pick them up at eleven for dinner which was served at noon.

He knocked at the door.

She had butterflies in her stomach and felt like a schoolgirl on her first outing with her beau. *This is silly. I've been a married woman and yet I never felt this way with Douglas. I don't know what's the matter with*

me. Being courted by Adam seems so much more...
important.

She opened the door, and Adam stood there looking better than a man had a right to look. He was dressed in denim pants and a white shirt with the sleeves rolled up, exposing strong forearms that made her warm. She practically had to fan herself.

"Adam, thank you for coming for us. We could have walked but I'm afraid we'd have been covered with mud by the time we arrived."

"I don't mind. It gives me that much more time alone..." He glanced at the children standing next to her. "Well, almost alone with you."

"They have promised to be very good today." She gazed down at her children. "Isn't that right you two?"

They both nodded.

"Are you ready for a buggy ride?" he asked the children.

"Yes, sir," said Larry.

Patty kept her thumb in her mouth but nodded.

"Let's get this party started."

Adam smiled at the kids and then held out his arm for Karen.

"I'd like to, but I need to carry Patty."

She bent and picked up her daughter, propping her on her hip while she walked to the buggy. The mud made the path very slippery and Karen thought she would fall, but Adam was there to steady her.

When they arrived at the buggy, Adam took Patty and put her on the backseat.

"Scoot over little darlin'," said Adam. "Your brother is coming back there, too."

Then it was Larry's turn and finally Adam helped Karen into the carriage.

He treats the children so well. Douglas was like that, too, with Larry when he was little. Something Adam and Douglas have in common.

"Everybody ready?"

Her children gave him a resounding chorus of "Yes!" in response. With a chuckle, he clicked his tongue and slapped the reins on the horse's flanks to start them walking. As soon as the buggy was clear of the town, Adam slapped the reins on the horses again and they broke into a trot. He kept them at that gait until they reached Jason's, which was the family home where Adam and Drew and Lucy still lived. His other two brothers, Gabe and Michael, had homes of their own, with their wives and children.

But on Saturday and Sunday, Jason's house was home for everyone.

Karen liked that about the Talbots. From her conversations with Rachel and Lucy, she knew the Talbot brothers had strong family values and a closeness she envied. She'd never been close to her sisters, Jolene and Felicia. They were much older, had small children when Karen was born and were more like aunts than sisters.

Douglas was an only child so had no family to speak of. A couple of distant cousins who lived in Maine and she'd never met.

"Karen?"

Adam waved a gloved hand in front of her, bringing her back to the here and now.

"Oh, I'm sorry. I was just thinking how much I envy you your family. I've got a couple of much-older sisters, but no one close."

"We are close. That's one reason all of us came out here when Jason decided to try his luck here in Seattle. That was almost eleven years ago. Billy was practically a newborn and our sister Suzanne was horrified that Jason would consider taking the baby. She told him to leave Billy with her and her new husband to raise. Jason flat-out refused and purchased passage on the Bonnie Blue to Seattle."

Karen enjoyed the ride. The buggy had springs and so was quite comfortable to ride in. "I can understand your sister's position. I'd have felt the same way if he'd been my brother. That's a very hard trip with an infant."

"It's not so bad when you have five fathers taking care of him. Jason did most of the work, but when he needed a break, we were there for him."

Karen tilted her head and gazed at Adam. He'll make a wonderful father. He already has the experience and great instincts where her children are concerned.

71

"When I've seen him at church, Billy is a wonderful boy. I'd say you all did a great job raising him."

Adam smiled. "I remember all the times we've caught him doing something he wasn't supposed to, like bringing a snake into the house in his pocket. If he did it now, Rachel would have his hide nailed to the door."

Karen laughed. "A snake."

"Was Billy bad?" asked Larry from the back seat. "We like Billy. He plays with us whenever he comes to town with his mama and he gives us candy sticks that he says come from Adam."

Karen thought about correcting him and telling him that Rachel wasn't Billy's mama, but she knew Larry wouldn't understand and Rachel would be pleased with the statement.

"He wasn't really bad," said Adam. "Just mischievous. He liked to have fun and that didn't always coincide with the brother's wants or needs."

"Why do you call yourself and your siblings 'the brothers'?"

"Our sister Suzanne started it. It's much easier and faster than naming them individually, especially since she was usually referring to all of us. We all use the word."

Karen heard the birds chattering in the trees. That was one more thing she liked about Seattle. The wildlife, whether birds, wolves, deer and elk. Even a bear or two was known to come into town.

"Tell me about your cousin, Ethan. Is he usually so forward and persistent?"

Adam's demeanor changed from friendly and affable to grumpy, almost angry.

"I don't know. I haven't seen him in more than ten years. He still acts like the spoiled boy he was then. He has way more money than he has sense."

"He's wealthy?" *An interesting fact.*

His head swiveled toward her, and his brows furrowed.

"He is. Does that make a difference?"

She crushed her skirt in her hands. "Not to me. I had a passing thought to approach him about loaning me the money for the clinic."

"You should stay away from him. As I said, he still acts the spoiled child. Who knows what lengths he'll go to in order to get what...or who...he wants."

She wanted to salute him. He sounded like a general giving orders to his troops. "Warning received loud and clear. Stay away from Ethan."

Adam visibly relaxed. As he did, so did Karen. She hadn't realized the mention of Ethan would upset him so, but she would try to avoid both the subject and the man.

They arrived at the house. Adam set the brake and came around to help Karen down.

Instead, he scooped her into his arms and deposited her on the bottom step of the stairs leading to the porch. He did the same with Larry and Patty. *Douglas would never have thought of carrying me so I didn't get muddier. Of course, he wasn't as strong as Adam.*

"Go on in. I'll be there after I care for the horses."

Karen smoothed the wrinkles she'd caused when she crushed the material and then walked to the door and knocked. The children followed.

Within just a few moments, the door swung wide and Billy stood in the opening wearing a grin.

"Hi, Mrs. Martell. Can Larry and Patty come play with me in the barn? We always have kittens."

Karen looked down at her children. "Would you like that?"

Larry nodded. "Yes, Mama. We'd like to a lot."

"All right, but you mind Billy so you don't get hurt. And Billy," her gaze settled on the boy. "I expect you to watch out for them. Okay?"

"Oh, yes, ma'am. I'll take care of them."

"You can go but come back when you're called for dinner."

"Yay!" yelled Larry as he and Patty followed Billy out the door.

Karen smiled and shook her head. *Kids.*

She went into the kitchen and found a hubbub of activity. Lucy and Rachel were both cooking or preparing dishes.

"Hi. Can I help?"

Lucy turned from the sink. "You sure can. I need help with these potatoes."

Lucy with her black hair was a beauty. A pregnant beauty. Karen guessed her baby would be there in about six or seven weeks.

"Do you have an extra apron?"

Rachel went to the pantry and brought out an apron made of heavy cotton.

"This should keep that pretty pink dress clean. Would you like a glass of iced tea?"

"No, thanks. How is Abbie?" Karen asked as she tied the apron behind her back.

Rachel's face lit up at the mention of her newborn daughter. "She's wonderful. Jason and I are so proud of her. Just a few weeks old and she's almost sleeping through the night. She only wakes up twice to be fed and changed."

Karen decided not to disabuse her of the notion that Abbie's sleep habits were special. She could sleep mostly through the night in a couple of weeks from then, but likely not yet.

Karen took the paring knife Lucy handed her and grabbed a potato. "That's wonderful. How many of these are we peeling?"

"Let's see." Lucy touched her chin. "There will be sixteen of us for dinner, but five of those are Talbot men and one is almost a Talbot man. I don't know about Ethan's appetite yet, as he's not been around for dinner or supper. And he sleeps way past breakfast. I assume he's eating at the hotel's restaurant. For now, though, we'll need twenty-five to be on the safe side."

Karen widened her eyes. *The cost to feed these men must be enormous.* "Oh, my. I never thought about what it takes to feed this many people, especially when they are Talbot men."

"Yes, preparing meals can be quite the undertaking." Rachel laughed.

Nicole and Michael walked in from the living room.

"How are you two?" Rachel greeted them both with hugs.

"We're wonderful." Nicole smiled and took Michael's arm and leaned into him.

Karen was surprised they'd made the journey since they lived so far away. She also noticed that Rachel, as Jason's wife, was definitely 'Mistress of the Manor'. She greeted everyone, made sure they got a glass of iced tea, sent the men to the porch and commandeered the women to help prepare the meal.

"Jason is in his office. The rest of the men are on the porch." Rachel jutted her chin toward the door to the rear of the kitchen at the end of the counter.

There were actually two doors there. One led to the office and one to the back porch.

"Michael, you go on. I'll bring you a glass of tea in a minute," said Nicole. "I'll help these ladies prepare our food."

"Don't let her near the stove unless it's to make Rachel's biscuits," teased Michael.

Nicole swatted him on the arm. "For that remark, you can come get your own tea."

Michael pouted and then laughed. He walked up to his wife and ran his finger down her nose. "I love you, Mrs. Talbot."

"I love you, too," the three women answered.

Karen chuckled. Their response was as though they'd prepared the line for a play.

Michael reddened, gave Nicole a kiss and high-tailed it out of the kitchen.

Nicole turned on her sisters-in-law. "You two are evil, teasing him like that." Then she giggled. Michael had done well with Nicole. Having been abused as she was, the fact that she was now able to share her grief, laugh if she wanted and there were no repercussions for either.

Nicole glanced Karen's way. "Why, Karen." She came over and hugged her. "What are you doing here?"

Karen stood a little straighter. "I came with Adam."

Nicole's eyebrows shot up. "Adam? Really?"

Karen grinned. "Yes, really."

"Well, this is an unexpected turn of events."

Karen looked away so Nicole wouldn't see her blush. "I don't know what you're talking about."

"Just that you seemed very interested last time Michael and I saw you. What was that, about a month ago? At the mercantile. You remember."

"Very interested in what?" asked Adam as he entered the kitchen from outside.

"Nothing," said Karen. "Are you done with the horses? I think the rest of the men are on the porch now. Rachel has iced tea ready. Would you like a glass?"

Adam tilted his head and stared with one eyebrow cocked. "Yes, iced tea would be nice."

Karen wiped her hands on a dish towel and poured Adam's tea. Then she handed him his glass. "Are you going outside?"

"I might find the conversation in here more interesting." He took a sip.

"If you stay here," Rachel put one hand on her hip and pointed at him with the other. "No further conversation will take place."

He grinned. "Ah, so you *were* talking about me."

"They could have been talking about me. My dear Karen. You look radiant today." Ethan walked up to her, took her hand, and kissed the top.

She pulled back her hand. "You must stop doing that."

"Why? You might change your mind about me. I'm really very gallant and quite the catch, or so I'm told."

Lucy rolled her eyes and mumbled under her breath. "Nothing wrong with his ego."

To keep from smiling, Karen bit her lip.

Ethan was not fazed, if he heard Lucy.

And Lucy was right. Something was *smug* about Ethan. She didn't trust him as far as she could throw him.

Adam put his arm around Ethan's shoulders and herded him out of the kitchen. "Come with me, young cousin. I'm sure you'll find our conversations as stimulating as the one happening here."

Ethan looked up at his cousin. "Somehow, I doubt it." He winked at Karen. She shook her head and turned away.

The man was impossible. She glanced Adam's way and saw him glowering at his cousin and opening and closing his fist. *Jealous.* Adam was jealous and though it shouldn't, the knowledge pleased her.

CHAPTER 7

Dinner was wonderful. The food was great and the conversation lively. Her children behaved well, much to her delight. She was proud of them.

"Can I help clean up?" she asked.

Rachel and Lucy eyed each other.

"Not this time." Rachel picked up the dishes from the table.

Karen was amazed that the bowls, once heaping with food were now empty.

Lucy took the hot water from the stove and poured it in a pan in the sink. "Next time you can assist. Why don't you and Adam take a walk? The weather is lovely for this time of year. We've had so much rain this winter. This is the first sunny day in…well I don't remember when."

Adam stood. "I think that's a marvelous idea." He helped Karen out of the chair next to him and then offered her his arm.

"Why don't I come with you? You can show me the property, too." Ethan hurried to push back his chair and stand.

Karen sure as heck didn't want Ethan to accompany her and Adam. She looked at Rachel and Lucy, silently pleading for help.

Rachel shook her head. "I think Jason has something he needs to talk to you about. Isn't that right, dear?" She jutted her chin toward Jason and furrowed her brows.

Jason walked over to Ethan and placed an arm on his shoulders. "Uh, yes, I have to talk to you in the office. Why don't you come with me?" He kept his arm on Ethan as they walked, mumbling something about an investment opportunity.

Adam smiled and settled her arm in the crook of his elbow. "Shall we?"

"We shall." Karen turned to Rachel. "Will you keep an eye on the kids? I'm sure Billy is entertaining them. They love playing with him. But in case they want me, tell them I'll be back after a bit."

Rachel smiled and scooped her hands in front of her, shooing them out the door. "Sure thing. Now go, before someone else wants something."

Karen laughed. "We're going." When they were outside and headed for the forest, she looked up at him. "We never did tell them we're courting."

He chuckled. "I believe they know."

"I suppose you bringing me to the family dinner, with my children, would be a big hint."

They crossed the yard and followed a path into the forest. The trees on either side were so thick, she could easily get lost if not for the foot trail.

They walked quietly for a while. Karen was surprised she didn't feel the need to fill the silence with empty words about the weather.

"When would you like to see me again?" asked Adam. "I'd like to see you every Saturday. Now that we're courting, I won't be at the family dinners for both Saturday and Sunday. I'll be doing things with you and the children. I do hope to include them most of the time, but on certain occasions I will want to see you alone. Does that schedule meet with your approval?"

She is thrilled he thought of this plan. "I haven't been courted in so long I don't know what I'm supposed to do. But I definitely want to see more of you alone. I love my children. They are my number one priority, but having a conversation with an adult who is not a patient is something I crave."

He patted her hand where it lay on his arm. "I'm happy to provide that service anytime."

"Where are we walking to?"

"A little meadow is up here with a small stream. We can be sure to be alone and I can take your beautiful face in my hands and kiss you."

She was sure her cheeks, heck her whole face, turned red.

"I'd like that very much." She whispered almost unable to get the words past the lump in her throat. Why did she feel like swooning because a man wanted to kiss her? She looked around. "We're alone and I would rather not wait. Kiss me now, Adam."

He stopped their progress toward the meadow and using the meager sunlight that shone through the trees, he cupped her face and lowered his.

She wrapped her arms around his neck and enjoyed her first kiss in years. Karen didn't know if her racing pulse was because he knew how to kiss or that she simply hadn't had one in so long.

His lips were soft and firm, gentle against her kiss-starved lips.

She wanted more. Wanted the kiss to be carnal, because that was how she felt. She cupped the back of his head and slowly pulled him tighter to her. Then she pressed her tongue against his lips and, thankfully, was rewarded with his tongue greeting hers. She felt alive, more than she had in years. Her body fairly hummed.

They kissed like that for a couple of minutes until Adam broke it off.

"If we don't stop now, I won't be able to control myself and I'll want, no need, to take you right here, right now."

She giggled. "We can't do that and you know it. Everyone would know exactly what we'd been doing because we'd be covered in mud and grass.

"I know and I don't care."

"Well, I do. I can't have my patients thinking me a loose woman, so…" She reached up and cupped his handsome jaw. "We are stopping now, before we both get lost in the moment."

"You're right. Shall we return?"

"Yes. Much to my disappointment. I'll be glad when we don't have to worry about getting carried away."

He held her by the waist, their lower bodies meshed together and she couldn't mistake his desire for her.

She was heady with the knowledge, because she wanted him, too. She hadn't had a man in her bed in much too long and she looked forward to reliving the experience. Douglas had been a good lover, because he'd been her only lover and she'd enjoyed the act.

Wondering if Adam would be a good lover, she stepped back and looked into his face. Unable to see his eyes, she didn't know if he'd enjoy her love making or not, but whatever he wanted she'd do her best to give him.

Karen knew she'd already fallen for Adam. That had happened even before he began to court her. She loved the way he interacted with his brothers, his ready smile and laugh. She loved that he brought her food when she was unable to get away to make her own, the way he simply took care of her.

And the way he interacted with the children, not just hers but all of the children in town. It wasn't unusual for him to buy candy sticks for each child and then send Billy to deliver them.

She looked up at him, though his face was in shadows and she couldn't see his eyes. "You're a nice man, Adam Talbot."

"I don't know how nice I am. I'm certainly having thoughts of you that no one would consider nice."

Smiling, she lowered her gaze and was glad for the camouflage of the thick foliage blocking the sunshine, so he couldn't see her reaction. "Now you're just being naughty."

"Exactly my point. When I look at your beautiful face, I want to be naughty...but only with you."

He cupped her face with his palm and lowered his head to hers. "Only with you." His lips touched hers with such reverence, she barely felt them. The kiss was soft, gentle and though nice, not at all what she wanted.

Suddenly he mashed his lips to hers, coaxed her tongue to meet his.

Then they danced, their tongues doing what their bodies couldn't. Meshing, dueling, loving.

Finally, she pulled back, her breathing ragged.

He didn't appear to be in any better shape.

She kept her eyes closed wanting the roar of wild emotions to continue. Wanting to etch this moment in her mind as the memory of her first kiss with Adam. The first of many, many more, if she had anything to say about it.

"Oh my."

He pulled her back into his arms and rested his forehead against her.

"Oh my, yes. I knew you were passionate, I didn't know just how much. But you had to have passion inside you to care for the people like you do and I hoped against hope your enthusiasm would extend to us. And it does. I'm well pleased."

"Me, too. That kiss was amazing."

"I should take you back before they send the dogs out to find us."

She chuckled. "They'd find us faster if they sent my children. They seem to know just when I don't want to be disturbed, in which case they have to talk to me right this minute."

They began the walk back to Jason's, this time holding hands.

"Billy used to do the same, but with five of us caring for him, he often didn't know which of us to 'bother' first. When he was a little younger than Patty, that meant standing in the living room and yelling until we all came. Needless to say, Jason had to break him of that habit."

"How do you discipline children?" She needed this answer more than anything else they'd talked about. She wouldn't put her children in the hands of someone who would beat them.

"If you're asking if I smack a child on the butt if he's in danger, yes, I would. But I don't believe in beating a child or spanking him or her to the point of tears. My father did that." His body stiffened. "I vowed I'd never treat my children that way."

"Isn't the child usually already crying just from the threat of a spanking?"

"Yes. But I got it in my head that I would not cry and he beat me, until I did."

His hand tightened around hers, as if drawing strength.

"It was a matter of power with him. He had to be the winner in our tests of wills. All I wanted was for him to love me. Turned out, he couldn't love any of us. Not really. He never wanted children, but he wouldn't or couldn't stay away from mother. She was a beautiful woman." He brought her hand to his lips and kissed the top. "Like someone else I know."

This man certainly knew how to make her blush.

"One thing I can say for him is he never struck her. Never hurt a hair on her head. I think if he had, we'd have killed him, the brothers and I."

He said it with a lack of emotion. To him it was a fact.

Karen stopped walking and hugged him. "I'm so sorry you had to grow up like that."

"I'm not. I know what being a bad parent is and know that I want to be a good one. I love kids. All of us do. Perhaps that's why we dote on Billy so much. Don't get me wrong, he's a little spoiled, but he shares everything he has with the other children in town. For instance, he shares the candy I buy him with all the other kids. Has been doing so since he was about six."

"That's pretty amazing in a six-year-old child. I'm glad he continues as a twelve-year-old boy."

He kissed her forehead and then stepped away, but took her hand in his.

"Come on. We need to go back or the family will begin to talk. I won't have anyone, including me, besmirching your reputation."

I don't think I've ever had anyone care about my reputation before. I kind of like it. "All right. I think that's probably a good idea, before I let you…heck, before I encourage you…to sully my reputation."

Adam brought her hand to his lips and kissed the top. "May I see you tomorrow? Perhaps we could take the kids and have a picnic somewhere. I know of a little lake not far from here. It's pretty and the children could fish and wade while you and I watch and talk."

They walked hand-in-hand through the trees. The closer they got to the end of the path, the lighter it got, until the sunlight shone bright.

"You'll have to teach the kids to fish. They've never learned nor have I." *The last time I was on a picnic was with Douglas. He'd asked me to marry him.*

"I can do that. I'm pretty good."

"I hope you are very patient as well."

"I am. You'll see we'll all have a great time."

When they returned to the house, everyone was gathered in the kitchen for dessert.

Rachel looked up when they walked in. "You're just in time. Lucy has baked her first cake."

Lucy added, "With Rachel's guidance, of course."

Rachel waved off the comment. "I only provided the recipe."

"That looks terrific." Drew placed a chaste kiss on his wife's brow.

"Before you all devour that lovely cake, I want to announce that..." Adam looked down at Karen and smiled. "Karen has agreed to let me court her. If all goes well we'll marry. Of course, we'd like your blessing."

The room erupted with shouts of "about time" and "good for you" and "congratulations".

Karen was pleased when each of the brothers gave her a hug. And then Rachel, crying, hugged her tightly. "Welcome to the family."

Nicole, also had tears in her eyes. "I wondered if he'd ever take the initiative."

"I heard that," said Adam with a smile. "I'm slow."

"I'll say," said Lucy. "Karen's had her eye on you since New Bedford. We brides had plenty of time to talk about the handsome Talbot brothers on the long sea voyage."

He turned to Karen. "Is that true? Since New Bedford?"

She nodded. "You fascinated me as much then as now."

"Me, too." He gave a single shake of his head. "I mean, you mesmerized me then, too."

"Well, isn't this just the perfect scene of bliss?" sneered Ethan, as he entered from the living room.

"What's the matter with you?" asked Jason.

Adam cocked an eyebrow and jutted his chin toward Ethan. "He thought he had a chance to know her."

"But...I made it perfectly clear when he asked me to dinner. Handsome though he is, he's much too young," sputtered Karen.

"Young!" Ethan spread his legs and fisted his hands at his sides. "I'll have you know I'm twenty-five and completely grown."

Karen stepped out of Adam's embrace and walked to Ethan. She laid a hand on his arm. "I'm thirty-two. That's much too old for someone your age. I don't mean you aren't a man, just that you're too young for me."

Ethan raised a hand and cupped her cheek.

She immediately pulled away from his touch.

He dropped his hand. "We'll never know, now will we?"

He turned and walked out of the room.

Karen stared after him in amazement and shook her head. "How very odd. He was insulted that I thought him too young."

Adam came up behind her and placed his hands lightly on her shoulders.

"Ignore him. Come. Let's have some of Lucy's cake and celebrate."

Karen reached up and squeezed one of Adam's hands. "Yes. Let's. I'm sure Lucy's cake, uh what kind is it, Lucy?"

"It's a plain yellow cake with chocolate frosting. I followed Rachel's instructions to the letter, so I take no blame if it's horrible."

They called the kids in and served them first, letting them take it back to the living room.

The cake wasn't horrible. It was terrific, with a moist interior and thick chocolate frosting.

"Thank you, Lucy. I know you didn't know today would be a celebration, but the dessert is perfect anyway." Karen ate the final bite of her cake.

Rachel suddenly looked toward the ceiling.

"Abbie's awake. If you'll excuse me."

She hurried out of the room.

With the quiet around the table, they all heard the baby, hollering at the top of her lungs. She wasn't very loud, though, but Rachel, being her mother had heard the sound of her daughter in distress.

A mother's instinct.

Would Karen still have the instinct to hear her baby's cry when she and Adam had children? What if he decided, after courting her a while, he didn't want to marry? Or what if they did marry and her children didn't accept Adam as their new father? What would she do then?

CHAPTER 8

Karen dressed with care in her maroon suit with the sweetheart neckline and the jacket that buttoned under her breasts.

She'd apparently put on some weight since she'd last worn this dress. Barely able to button the jacket, she examined herself in the mirror. The garment still looked good. She was wearing it to talk to Jason Talbot about funding her clinic. When she saw the amount of cleavage showing, she jammed her breasts down lower in the corset until she was satisfied with the result. Then she put on her ruby necklace, the last piece of jewelry Douglas bought her.

Karen wished she'd asked Adam to bring the buggy and take her up to the house, but she hadn't thought of needing a ride and now was faced with the walk in the mud. Oh well, there was nothing for it except to get started.

She'd put a sign on her door that she was away until one o'clock. She thought that would give her enough time to talk to Jason, get back and changed before the first patient showed up. The children were with Alice, so they were safe.

Quinn was outside waiting for her.

"I'll walk with you. I'm not to let you out of my sight, remember?"

"I do. Shall we go?"

They headed out to the Talbot home about a twenty minute walk, mostly uphill after leaving town.

Quinn kept at her side, shortening his stride to match hers.

They arrived and climbed the steps to the porch. Before she knocked she smoothed her skirt and patted her hair in place.

"I'll leave you now, but I'll be back in the waiting room when you return."

"I appreciate that. Thank you for escorting me."

He tipped his hat. "Certainly."

She knocked and Adam opened the door, a wide smile on his face. Slowly, his smile changed to a frown. His eyebrows furrowed and his eyes narrowed.

"What are you doing here like that?"

What's the matter with him? How could he change so quickly? "Like what?

He waved his hand up and down in front of her. "Wearing that dress? Are you thinking of seducing

Ethan before we marry? Decided his money would be easier to get?"

She gasped and her stomach clenched. "Adam, I don't know what you're talking about. This is my best suit. What's the matter with the way it looks that would have you so upset?"

He stood stiff and pointed at her bodice. "Your breasts are exposed for everyone to see, and all that creamy white skin, set off with that necklace pointing directly at your cleavage."

During the walk up the hill, her breasts shifted and she was now showing all the cleavage she'd tried to hide.

He stepped forward and pinned her to the wall with his hands on either side of her head.

"You're just like Phoebe—"

"Who's Phoebe? Why are you acting like this?"

"My ex-fiancée. Just like her you're interested in a man if he has money. Well, I've got money. Let's just get to the wedding night, without the wedding, what do you say?"

He lowered his head and tried to kiss her.

Karen turned away and struggled to get out of his hold. "Stop. Adam you don't know what you're doing."

When he let go of one arm, she formed a fist and punched him in the face.

Adam smiled, gathered her into his embrace, pinning her arms at her sides.

"Come on. Give me a kiss. I'm as good as anyone. We'll stop courting and I'll give you what you want."

"Adam, please, stop." She struggled and kept turning her head back and forth as he leaned close to kiss her.

"Adam!"

Jason's voice shattered the scene.

Adam looked up. "Go away. I'm just giving her what she wants."

Suddenly, she was free and Adam was flying over the porch railing. Jason stood above him on the porch looking down at his brother, lying in Rachel's flower garden.

"Come to my office. Now!"

He turned to Karen.

"I'm sorry. Please, let me help you to the office. We have things to discuss."

She couldn't believe what just happened. Why did Adam see his ex-fiancee when he looked at her now? He may have been hurt, but that doesn't excuse his behavior. Karen looked up at Jason. "I don't think I want to talk about funding the clinic right now."

"Nor do I. Come to the office, please."

She nodded once and went inside.

Jason escorted her through the house to the office.

Adam followed them, rubbing his arm.

She hoped it hurt.

"Please take a seat, both of you."

He pointed at the leather Queen Anne chairs in front of the desk.

"What happened out on the porch to cause the scene I came upon?"

Adam jutted his chin at Karen. "Let her tell you."

Karen took a deep breath. Her heart was breaking at the horrible side of Adam's personality. "Very well. I came here to discuss financing for my clinic with you, Jason. Adam seems to think I came with the intent to seduce Ethan."

"Why would he think that?"

Heat filled her cheeks, but she pressed on. "Because of the garments I'm wearing. Apparently, he thinks my best dress is inappropriate."

Jason looked at her for a minute.

"Even if that were true, your dress design doesn't explain his behavior."

Adam slumped in his chair and scrubbed his face with his hands.

"She reminded me of Phoebe. I thought she was here to get the money from Ethan."

Karen gazed at him.

He wouldn't look at her.

Jason steepled his fingers. "Didn't she tell you she was here to see me?"

Adam turned away and looked down at the floor.

"I thought she'd changed her mind."

Jason shook his head and took a deep breath.

"You have besmirched Karen's reputation. Lord, knows the men delivering the lumber for the house saw exactly what happened on the porch today. You have no other choice but to marry right away. If you don't and this event gets talked about, Karen will lose her patients, her practice and a clinic won't be needed. Do you understand me?"

Karen's mouth formed a thin line. *This can't be happening to me. How can I lose my love and my dream in one moment.* "I don't want to marry him."

"Unfortunately, Adam didn't leave either of you a choice if you wish to remain in Seattle."

"Jason." Adam leaned forward in the chair. "I'm sorry."

Jason frowned and waved his hand toward Karen.

"I'm not the one you need to apologize to."

Adam straightened and then ran his hand behind his neck.

She knew this movement happened whenever he was frustrated. *I thought I had a good man, but I don't like this ugly side.*

"Karen," he began. "I'm very sorry for manhandling you outside. I should have listened and not let my temper dictate my actions. Will you do me the honor of becoming my wife?"

She narrowed her eyes and leaned away from him. "No."

He reached over and took her hand in his.

"Karen, please. I'm so sorry. I know you're not like Phoebe. You're kind, gentle and care about people rather than yourself. I was blind for a moment, but I'm not anymore. Please, give me a second chance."

She didn't remove her hand, which hurt from hitting him. But he held her gently, she could have pulled back at any time and she doubted he would have stopped her. Looking up from her hands into his beloved face, she almost caved and accepted the marriage proposal completely. But she couldn't. Not wholly.

Karen took a deep breath. "Very well. We'll marry for appearance's sake. But that is all." She stiffened her spine. "We will not consummate this marriage any time soon. Perhaps not ever. You hurt me, Adam and shattered my trust in you." She retrieved her hand and placed it in her lap. "You'll have to rebuild that trust if you ever expect us to have a real marriage. Now if you'll excuse me, I want to go home. I've got patients to see." She stood and turned to leave.

Jason stood.

So did Adam.

"Karen," said Jason. "What about your clinic?"

She turned and looked from him to Adam.

"There's no point in building a clinic, until we find out if I will have any patients or if this marriage will work or not."

"It will work," Adam mumbled under his breath. "I'll make it work. You'll see."

"Yes, we will see." She looked up at Jason. "When do you want this wedding to take place?"

"Tonight." Jason crossed his arms over his chest. "The sooner the better. I'll talk to Reverend Peabody and see if he'll come for supper, like he did with Michael and Nicole."

Karen nodded. "I'd appreciate if you'd send someone with the buggy for the children and me."

Adam put his hands in his pockets. "I'll come get you as usual."

She didn't look at him. "If you must. We'll be ready at six-thirty if that meets with everyone's approval."

"We normally have supper at six. If you could be here about five-forty-five, that would be better," said Jason.

Karen merely nodded. Her thoughts in a whirl about the rapid changes in her life.

"I'll pick you up at five-thirty," said Adam.

"We'll be ready."

"Wait for a moment," said Adam. "I'll get the buggy to take you home."

"I'd rather walk. Thank you."

"You shouldn't. We haven't found the Jacobsen woman yet. Walking alone is too dangerous."

"I'm not alone. Quinn is with me and probably witnessed the whole debacle. But, I'm sure he wouldn't mind the ride. Jason, will you take us home. I have no desire to be in his company right now."

"Certainly." Jason frowned at Adam and slowly shook his head. He turned to Karen.

"You can accompany me to the barn if you like."

"I'll do that."

She walked out, back straight enough to be used as an ironing board.

Adam didn't follow her, for which she was glad. She dreaded the fact that her hoped for love was now in tatters. As it was, she cried—walked and cried.

Karen heard the buggy drive up at exactly five-thirty. Adam was nothing if not punctual. Karen opened the door before he could knock. All she wanted was to get this farce over with as soon as possible. She would not let him see her as anything but calm and aloof.

"We'll be right with you." She faked a smile and turned to her children. "Are you ready, my loves?"

"Yup," said Patty.

"Horses. We get to ride in the buggy again." Larry shot out the door and ran to the carriage.

Karen smiled. "He's excited about seeing the horses. He hasn't been able to talk about anything else since we came for family dinner."

The little boy ran to the horses and began to pet their soft noses.

"He loves those animals," observed Adam.

"He does. I'm surprised he didn't ask if he could bring them some sugar." She wrapped her reticule strings around her hand, took a deep breath and stiffened her spine. "Shall we go? I'd like to get this over with as soon as possible."

"No need to be so negative on our wedding day. We should just make the best we can out of a bad situation," grumbled Adam.

She gasped. "How can you call this a "bad situation" and not be negative about it?

"I tend to be an optimist. We were getting married anyway. This is just a bit sooner than either of us planned."

"I suppose that's correct. But I hate the way we have to marry and I blame you."

"I suppose it is my fault."

She turned her narrowed gaze on him. "Yes, it is. If you hadn't been so crazy jealous, this would never have happened this way."

"I know. I'm sorry. I won't make that mistake again."

"We'll see." She stared at the road headed up the hill and wondered what lay ahead for them.

When they arrived at Jason's, the living room had been set up for the ceremony. The sofa and chairs were moved to the sides so there was an aisle down the middle to the fireplace where Reverend Peabody stood.

Adam was on the reverend's left and Jason on Adam's left.

Rachel, acting as Karen's matron of honor, stood smiling on the reverend's right.

Karen approached down the makeshift aisle holding a small bouquet of wildflowers Billy had picked for her. When she was in place, Reverend Peabody cleared his throat and began to read.

"Dearly beloved we are gathered together to join this man and this woman in holy wedlock...Do you Adam John Talbot take this woman, Karen Evangeline Martell for your lawful wedded wife, to have and to hold from this day forward and to keep yourself only unto her for as long as you both shall live?"

"I do." Adam's voice rang out loud and clear.

The reverend turned toward Karen.

"Do you Karen Evangeline Martell take Adam John Talbot to be your husband and do you promise to love, honor and obey him and keep yourself only unto him for as long as you both shall live?"

"I...I..." Karen stopped. The words not coming, then she looked up at Adam. He looked at her, his blue eyed gaze never leaving hers to look at his family. He didn't show fear. He only smiled and nodded at her, giving her time to really make up her mind, to say the words on her own. Suddenly, she knew she couldn't turn him down. This wasn't her ideal situation to be married, but he was willing to try, so would she. "I do."

Her hand shook when Adam slid the plain gold band on her finger.

She couldn't believe he had a ring. He must have gotten it after...the incident. And the plain gold band was perfect for her. Karen would be able to wear it all the time, unlike a diamond ring, which she would have had to take off to do her work. She couldn't reach into a woman to turn a breach baby wearing a diamond ring. Karen was pleased. Whether Adam purchased the ring because he understood, or because it was the only one the mercantile had in stock, she didn't care. The ring was perfect for her.

Karen heard the reverend say, "You may now kiss your bride." She looked up at Adam who smiled, cupped her face between his palms, leaned down and touched her lips to his.

She thought that was all there would be and though disappointed, she started to pull back.

Adams fingers, wrapped around the back of her head, tightened and he brought her back to his lips. He deepened the kiss and when he pressed his tongue forward, she gave a little gasp of surprise and he pressed on, engaging her tongue, urging her to come and play.

She did, fulfilling one of her wishes. She wanted Adam to kiss her...really kiss her. And he was. Closing her eyes, she let her tongue be teased, her lips smashed, her heart soared for a moment, then the reality of the situation returned.

Finally, she and Adam heard the family clapping and broke apart. How long they had been making noise, trying to get her and Adam's attention, she had no idea, but if the smiles on the women and each of the brothers smacking Adam on the back, were any indication, it had been a while.

Karen felt the heat in her cheeks and wondered if Adam felt the same, but when she chanced to look at him, he was grinning at her and appeared to be very happy. Could he be?

After the ceremony, Adam took them all, his new family, home. Her house was his home now, too, though she'd be just as happy if he continued to live at Jason's. For appearance sake, he had to live here.

As soon as they entered the house he set his valise by the door.

She decided to put as much distance from Adam as possible. "Come, children, I'll help you to put on your pajamas and get ready for bed."

"Can't we stay up a little longer?" whined Larry. "I want to play marbles with Adam."

She put her hands on her hips. "No. If you don't stop addressing me with that tone in your voice, you'll get no milk and cookies."

He hung his head. "Yes, Mama."

"That's better. Let's go."

Karen came out of the children's room and headed toward the kitchen, where she set the table with the children's treats.

Finally she turned to Adam who sat at the table. "Would you like milk and cookies or can I interest you in a cup of coffee or tea?"

"Milk and cookies, please. I do have a sweet tooth but the time is much too late for coffee or tea."

She had to smile at his reasoning, but she agreed. She usually enjoyed the treat with the children.

Karen prepared two more settings before the children returned.

"Everyone sit and enjoy. After this, it's bedtime." She said the same thing to the children every night reminding them what comes next. A story. Usually she didn't get any lollygagging before story time.

Adam lifted an eyebrow and grinned.

Karen narrowed her eyes and frowned. "We'll talk later."

"Yes, ma'am. We will."

"Mama, since you and Adam got married will he live here now?" asked Larry with a mouth full of cookie.

"Don't speak with your mouth full. Swallow first." She admonished him.

"In answer to your question, yes Adam will live here from now on." *My bedroom is hardly big enough for a pallet on the floor, but he'll have to make do.*

Larry frowned and his eyes teared up. "Is he gonna be my new daddy? I don't want a new daddy."

"Oh, honey," She went to Larry's side and knelt to the boy's eye level. "I'm sure once you get used to Adam being here, you'll be very glad to have him as your daddy. Didn't you have fun when we went on our picnic yesterday?"

He nodded. "Uh huh."

"Well, we can do that more often now and other things, too. Adam can teach you how to ride a horse and many more things that I can't."

Larry looked over at Adam, his mouth in a thin line.

She'd never seen her son this angry and was at a loss for words to soothe him. If she and Adam had continued with a regular courtship, this problem with Larry would never have come up.

Finally, his mouth softened. "Will you teach me how to ride? Can I have my own horse?"

Adam smiled. "I'll teach you everything I know. Everything you need to have fun and to grow up and be a good man. As to a horse, your mama and I will have to make that decision, when the time is right."

Larry furrowed his brows for a moment. "Okay. But I'm not calling you Daddy. You're *not* my daddy."

"You're right I'm not, but I like to think your father would approve of me." He glanced her way.

She cocked a brow, incredulous. *How could he believe Douglas would ever approve of him after his behavior this morning?* And mouthed, "Really?"

"I want to help you and your mother. She works too hard and can't spend as much time with you as she'd like. I want to help her to spend more time with you."

The boy's eyes opened wide. "You do?"

"I do."

Karen watched Adam interact with her son. He was gentle with the little boy's fearful feelings. Fear of losing a father he barely remembered but more so of losing his mother. That Adam would calm her son made her fall a little more in love with him. But that softening didn't mean she would let him into her bed. Not yet. Maybe not ever if he couldn't control his jealousy.

After the snack and getting the children into bed, the time had come for her and Adam to go to bed.

"I have a pallet made under the bed. I'll pull it out and you can sleep there. I'm not ready to let you into my bed."

He gazed at her for a moment and in the end nodded his head. "I understand and I don't suppose I blame you."

"That's the way it has to be. You don't trust me and until I have at least your trust, I'll not let you make love to me."

"Karen, I do trust you...I—"

"You don't. If you did we wouldn't find ourselves in this situation right now."

He sighed. "I suppose you're right. This is entirely my fault. I'm sorry. I know this is not how you imagined being married again."

"No, I didn't. None of this situation is the way I imagined our married life to begin, but since it has, you will follow my rules if you ever want to sleep in my bed. I prepared a pallet on the floor of my bedroom for you before we left. You'll have to sleep there."

"As you wish."

I don't want to do this. I want more than anything for Adam to make me his, to have a real marriage, but unless he changes that won't happen. Will he change? Am I putting too much faith in him, in the relationship, in us?

CHAPTER 9

The next day, Karen delivered a healthy baby boy. Even though she was tired, she was happy. Bringing a new life into the world was so satisfying. Six pounds twelve ounces and twenty inches long. Good sized considering his father was only five foot three inches and his mother just under five feet. He would be a giant compared to them.

Quinn had accompanied her as he always did when she walked about town. Her shadow until Anna Jacobsen was found.

By the time they arrived at her home, she was exhausted and still angry with Adam. How could he think she would try to seduce Ethan? Didn't he hear her on Saturday when she'd said he was too young? He was a handsome boy, but still a boy. She wanted a man. Adam was a man and being his wife, she could have relations with him whenever she pleased. But this is not the way she wanted to marry him. She needed him down on one knee, pledging his love and asking her to be his wife.

Girlish dreams. She knew better than to believe that her dreams might come true. She'd had her dreams fulfilled when young, to an extent. She wanted to be a doctor, but settled for being Douglas's wife. She'd wanted to go back to school after they married, but he wanted a wife that stayed at home and raised children, gave him a hot dinner and warmed his bed. So she'd become that which he wanted.

Not that she regretted having her children. She didn't. They were each one a blessing as far as she was concerned, and she wouldn't trade either one of them for all the gold in the world.

Just once, she'd like to have someone on her terms. Not because of what he wanted and certainly not just to save her reputation. Yes, she and Adam had agreed to begin courting, with marriage being the intended result, but they'd just begun. What if it turned out they hated each other?

She got to the house and noticed a note on the door. Looking around she wondered where Abe was. How could Anna have slipped by him?

"Quinn, find Abe. Find him fast."

Her heart hammered in her chest and her hands were suddenly clammy. This couldn't be good news. She'd never received any note this way except the threats from Anna Jacobsen. Was this another?

With hands shaking so badly she could barely hold on to the piece of paper, she opened the note.

I've taken what was mine. You'll never see her again and she's such a sweet, trusting little thing.

She heard a scream and realized it was coming from her.

Michael and Nicole Talbot came running out of the mercantile. Quinn and Abe came from around the back of the house.

Michael reached her first.

"Karen. Karen! What's wrong?"

"My baby!"

She pushed him aside and ran down the steps heading for Dormitory One.

"Alice! Alice!"

Larry met her at the door, crying.

"Alice is hurt, Mama. Some lady hit her with a shovel and then took Patty. I couldn't do anything. She took my sister, and I couldn't stop her."

Karen knelt and closed her arms around her son.

"It's all right, baby. We'll get Patty back. You be a big boy now and stay here with Nicole and Michael, while Mama checks on Alice."

"Okay." He sniffled.

Nausea threatened to make her vomit. Her stomach clenched. She looked up at Michael.

"Find Adam. Tell him what has happened. We have to find her before Anna Jacobsen disappears forever with my daughter."

Michael placed a hand on her shoulder and squeezed.

"We'll find her. I'll get Adam from work. We'll use every lumberjack, every townsman to search for her. Anna won't get away with this. Do you hear me, Karen?"

His words didn't bring much comfort, but she nodded. "I hear you. Where is Adam? I need Adam."

"I'll go get him. Nicole you stay here with her."

Nicole nodded. "I won't leave."

Michael kissed his wife and then ran toward his wagon parked outside the mercantile.

Karen checked Alice's wound. Luckily, Anna was short and Alice was tall. The shovel left a small gash in her head, but had mostly hit her shoulders and back.

After she treated Alice and stitched up the cut on her head, Karen went outside and sat on the steps to wait for Adam.

Nicole sat with her and put an arm around Karen's shoulders. "They'll get her back. The brothers won't stop until they find Patty."

Karen just sat there, tears streaming down her cheeks. Finally, numb from crying, she didn't think she had anymore tears but when she saw Adam, fresh ones welled in her eyes.

Adam galloped up and jumped off before the horse even stopped.

She ran down the steps and threw herself into his waiting arms.

"Anna, took her. She took Patty."

"I know." He hugged her close. Their differences of yesterday forgotten for now. "Michael, told me. I came as fast as I could."

She noticed the horse had no saddle. Adam had ridden him bareback, to save time.

"The brothers are gathering the men. All work has stopped. Jason will go by the mill and tell Alfred Pope what has happened and ask that his men join in. I'm sure they will.

"We will go door to door. Search every cabin, every flop house, every hotel and inn. We'll find them."

She leaned back and grabbed onto the front of his shirt. "You have to. You just have to."

Adam pulled her back into his embrace. He was so warm and she was so cold even though the weather was mild for this time of year. Cold from the inside out, she shook and her teeth chattered.

"I'm in shock. I can't stop shaking."

Adam turned and looked at Nicole. "Take her home and pour her a hot bath, then put her to bed."

"What about you?" asked Nicole.

"I'm finding that bitch before she can get Patty aboard a ship and we lose her forever."

"With so many ports, how will you stop her?"

Nicole's voice was steady and she asked the questions Karen wanted to but couldn't.

"We're sending a man to each town and talking to every captain that will be leaving in the next three days. Those are only the closest ones and she won't get farther afield than that."

"Adam." Karen's voice shook and clenching her jaw to stop her teeth from chattering, made it difficult to speak. "She hasn't much money. She might...just check the whore houses, too."

He kept his arms around her. "Already on my list. Will you be all right until I get back?"

She looked up at him and shook her head. "I may never be all right again. Please find my baby. Please. Adam, I'll do anything. Anything she wants just give me back my baby." His warmth seeped into her and she let herself feel it.

He held her close. Didn't say anything but let her feel his warmth.

"Nicole will take you home and prepare a bath. Get in it and soak for a while until you can talk without breaking a tooth."

What is he thinking? She pulled out of his arms. "I d...don't have time to t...take a b...ba...bath."

He laid both his hands on her shoulders. "All right. Calm down. Just go home and have a nice cup of tea. Try to warm up."

She closed her eyes and nodded. "I'll do my best, but keep me informed. Please. Don't leave me wondering."

"As soon as I know something you'll be the second to know."

Karen's chest was tight and the lump in her throat threatened to rob her of speech. She realized as long as Adam was with her he wasn't looking for Patty. "Go. Bring Patty back. I don't care what you have to do."

He pulled her back into his embrace and kissed the top of her head. "I will. She's my daughter now, too. I won't let anything happen to her.

Adam gathered all his brothers and every employee outside the office of Talbot Lumber.

"Okay, men, we're looking for a three-year-old girl with dark brown hair in the company of a single woman. The woman is short, with mousy brown hair and tattered clothes. It is possible this woman has cut Patty's hair to look like a boy."

"Should we stop every woman?" asked Lars Hendrickson.

"Yes. Question every woman with a child who you don't know personally."

A murmur sounded from the men as they nodded and repeated what Adam said.

"I want this third of you to head south to Tacoma." He waived a hand toward the men on his left. "This third," he waved to the men on his right. "Will head north. The rest of you will canvass the area around Seattle and work your way east. I'll check as many of the outlying cabins east of here as I can.

"Okay, everyone return here by tomorrow night. Now, go. Find my daughter."

Jason came over to him, his eyebrows drawn together and mouth turned down at the corners. "Your daughter already? I think that's good."

"Those kids need a father and I want to be that person. So yes, she's my daughter."

Jason clapped him on the back. "I'm glad you're happy with your ready-made family."

Adam stood watching the men ride out. A hundred horses and men, took minutes to disperse. He turned to Jason. "I am. Very. I'll get Karen to come around, to forgiving me. I was a jealous fool."

"You were. But you have accepted the consequences. I know you intended to marry Karen anyway, but she will be a hard nut to crack. Rachel tells me, Karen is not happy with this marriage. She wanted the courting, you on one knee, and so forth."

"I know and I'll pay for my stupidity. I know that she loves me, if not now, then soon. When she knows, she'll let me make love to her."

"What about you? Do you love her?"

Adam frowned and looked away. "I'll never fall in love again. Phoebe took all of my love and stomped it into the dirt. I won't be that vulnerable."

Jason clapped him on the back. "You're wrong, little brother. Love makes you strong. You'll see."

Adam shook off his brother's hand. "Phoebe taught me all I need to know about love. It's not real. Now, lust. That's real."

Jason cocked an eyebrow. "So you're saying all you feel for Karen is lust?"

He crossed his arms over his chest. "Of course. Men don't fall in love. Women do. That's all there is to it."

His brother shook his head and frowned. "Don't tell me that all I feel for Rachel is lust, because I'll knock you down. I feel more love for her than I ever have anyone, including Cassie. *That* is what's real."

Adam put up his hands in front of him. "You and Rachel are a special case. All of you brothers are. I don't understand it, but that trait, the ability to fall in love skipped me. In any case, that isn't important right now. Patty is my only concern. We have to get her back."

"You're right. Let's go."

"I'm checking the old fishing hole and that cabin where Gabe and Josie found those kids. It's the closest to town and would be easy for Anna to hide in."

"The brothers and I will check the ones farther out. There are many of them. We won't get to them all before nightfall."

"I know and I don't want to have that little girl spending even one night in that woman's clutches."

Adam and Jason mounted their horses. He was proud and thankful his men were more than willing to help find the child. For the first time since before Phoebe jilted him, he prayed.

Karen sat in her kitchen with her sisters-in-law and baby, Abbie. She was envious of Rachel for having Abbie and she knew that was crazy, but she missed Patty so much. She wanted to hold Abbie, keep her close, but more than anything she wanted to hold *her* baby. Patty had to be scared out of her mind. Patty was not even three yet. Not until July. How could Karen let this happen? Why hadn't she been more protective of her children? *Because I thought Anna was after me, not my kids. Quinn and Abe have been watching me, not the children. And I thought they were safe with Alice and the other brides at the dormitory.*

"Karen. Would you like some tea?" Rachel nursed Abbie, with a cloth over her chest for privacy. "Karen." She snapped her fingers.

"Oh, I'm sorry. I should be offering you tea or I can make coffee. Water or milk, perhaps? I have them all. Patty is my milk drinker. She and Larry both love the stuff." Karen smiled at the memory. "But she'll try to get it for herself when she thinks I'm not looking. Why is it they always think we aren't watching them?" She paused and tears filled her eyes, threatening to spill over and join the rest on her cheeks.

Josie, Gabe's wife, reached over and squeezed Karen's hand.

"The brothers will find her, and when they do that woman better watch out. No one comes between the brothers and their kids. Trust me."

Karen gave Josie a small smile. "I know, but Patty isn't Adam's child. He called her his daughter, but I think that's Only for my benefit."

Josie held Karen's hand.

"You'd be surprised. I believe that Adam does think of your children as his. He wouldn't have taken you to our special fishing hole for your picnic on Sunday, if he didn't. He wouldn't have dropped everything at work and rushed to you, if he didn't."

Karen squeezed her eyes shut. Just for this minute, she believed Adam would keep looking for her daughter because he thought of her as his. He would bring her home.

She was full of hope but knew that the longer the search, the less likely she'd ever see Patty again.

Lucy stood and went around to the back of Karen's chair. She hugged her around the neck.

"Adam will be successful. You'll see."

Karen reached up and touched her own cheek. It was wet.

"I can't stop crying."

Lucy squeezed her one more time and then stepped back.

"You're all right. We understand and you're allowed to cry."

"Excuse me, I'll be right back."

As soon as she got to her bedroom, she sat on the edge of the bed, buried her face in her hands and wept. She realized her actions were accomplishing nothing. She needed to be positive. Crying did no one any good.

When she'd recovered, she rejoined the sisters-in-law. The beloved women were now a part of her family. She knew they only wanted to comfort her, but didn't they know, she only wanted to be alone in her grief.

No. They were right to be here. To keep her from giving up. To pray for the return of her daughter. And so she did. She prayed as she never had before. Patty had to come back. She just had to.

Dusk had fallen when Adam reached the abandoned cabin. He saw smoke coming from the chimney. He would have been surprised, if he wasn't sure Anna and Patty were inside. They had to be. He'd never been as afraid as he was for his little girl. Yes, Patty was his and all he wanted right now was to find her and ease the knot in his stomach.

He left his horse, hidden by the trees, and walked carefully toward the cabin, skirting the edge of the clearing, using the trees and shadows as camouflage. When he was directly across from the side of the cabin, he hurried to the dwelling and flattened himself against the wooden logs.

Hearing nothing coming from inside, he worked his way around to the door and tried the handle. It opened.

Chapter 10

Sitting in one of the two straight-back chairs in front of the fire was an older man who stirred something in a pot over the open flame and smoked a pipe.

Adam looked around the one room cabin and saw no one else. "Who are you?"

The man kept his eye on the pot. "Name's Seth Ely. You be a Talbot?"

Adam narrowed his gaze on the white haired old man. "I am. How do you know? I've never met you."

"She said you'd come. Said she had something you wanted real bad."

I'm on the right track. "You mean Anna Jacobsen?"

"Maybe. She didn't give me no name. Just her and the little girl was here when I came. She, Anna, you say, was packing up and getting ready to leave."

Adam stepped closer to the man who was just on the other side of the table. He still hadn't risen or even looked at Adam. "Where is she?"

He finally turned toward Adam. "She said to tell you, you'll never find her, so stop looking."

Posture rigid, Adam shook his head and hands fisted at his sides. "Never. She's got my daughter."

Seth took out his pipe. "Thought that might be the case. The girl didn't look nothing like the woman."

Adam stepped around the table. "Tell me, old man, where they went before I lose my temper."

"Sure." Seth put his hands up. "Ain't no never mind to me. She took off through the woods. She said she was headed for Tacoma but she went east. I figure she ain't got no idea where she's goin'."

"How long ago did she leave?"

"She's got a good two hours on you."

"When I find her she'll be sorry she ever crossed, Adam Talbot." Adam's voice was normal now, he didn't growl at the man. "Thank you for your help. Here," Adam handed him a twenty-dollar bill.

"Don't want your money, Mr. Talbot. I should have helped that little girl. But I didn't."

"Giving me the information is worth the money."

"That's mighty nice of ya, Mr. Talbot."

Adam held out his hand to the old man. "I'm pleased to meet you, Seth Ely. You've helped me get my daughter back and that's worth the world to me."

"I'd have stopped her if I'd known." He took a long draw off his pipe.

"Thank you for that. I'll be back by here after I get Patty."

Seth nodded.

"You're welcome anytime. Anytime at all."

Adam turned and left the cabin. *She's taking her through the woods. She'll have to go over the slide. I'll catch her then.*

Karen leaned against the kitchen door jamb and watched Larry play. His mind didn't seem to be on the game of marbles because his steelie marble kept going over the string. He was upset and she needed to comfort him as best she could.

She walked into the living room and sat across the circle from him on the floor after arranging her skirts so they'd be out of the way.

"Hi, baby. How are you doing?"

He looked up, his eyes narrowed and his mouth in a thin line.

"What's the matter, baby?"

"Don't call me that. I'm not a baby."

"Okay, I won't if the name upsets you so. But, you know, you'll always be my baby. My first born.

Special. No matter how old you get, that fact can't change."

She watched him struggle with wanting to be comforted and trying to be strong. She opened her arms wide and didn't say another word.

He stood and ran across the string circle for his marbles and jumped into his mother's embrace, where he burst into tears.

"Everything will be fine." She held him tight. "Adam will find Patty. You'll see. She'll be home soon. They both will."

He looked up at her, tears staining his chubby cheeks.

"I didn't mean it when I said I don't want another daddy. I was scared."

She took the hanky from her sleeve and wiped his tears. "What were you afraid of?"

"That because you're married to Adam, you won't have time for me and Patty."

She hugged him close, one arm around his waist and the other around his back with her hand cupping his head.

"I'll always have time for you two. You're my children and that will never change. Adam knows you mean the world to me and he wants to be your father. He loves you and Patty."

Now if he could just love me, too.

A knock sounded.

She set Larry away from her, to answer the door.

"Jason!"

She looked around him for Patty, but only saw her new brothers-in-law. Her shoulders fell.

"You don't have her."

"No, we couldn't find hide nor hair of her or Anna. They haven't gone to Tacoma or anywhere south or north. Our last hope is Adam. He headed east. We didn't really think she would go that way. The travel is through forests and very hard, even without a child."

Karen put fingers on her temple, the other hand at her hip and paced in a circle in front of Jason. "This woman is crazy. I doubt she knew or, if she did, that she cares how hard the travel is. If she did, she wouldn't have tried it with a child in tow."

The brothers and, to her surprise, Ethan, filed into the living room from the porch. Jason stayed with her. The other men dipped their heads as they passed on the way to the kitchen.

Jason stood in front of her. "You have the right of it."

"I'm sorry. Where are my manners? I should offer you some coffee and food. The ladies have made supper and kept it hot for you all. The rest of us have eaten."

Jason stopped her pacing by placing his hands on her shoulders. "You don't have to play hostess. We're family now. We are all as angry about the kidnapping as you, even though we haven't known Patty very well. She's just a baby, after all."

Karen smiled, though she doubted it reached her eyes because she was anything but happy. "She and Larry both hate that I call them that. They want so much to be grown up already. Except when they're hurt, or hungry, or sleepy. You know what I'm talking about. I'm sure you went through much the same with Billy."

Jason chuckled. "We went through that, but Billy had it worse. He had the five of us all calling him 'baby'. He would get so mad, it was almost comical to watch."

Karen nodded. "Thank you for trying to cheer me up. I'll have more cheer than any one will want when Patty is returned."

"I understand. Come with me to the kitchen and be with your family."

Jason led the way to Karen's kitchen where her new sisters-in-law and the other three brothers-in-law and Ethan waited.

She was surprised by Ethan's presence.

"Thinking of you as family is so new. Family. I still think of you as my friends."

"Hopefully, we can be both," said Jason.

As they entered, Rachel came forward, carrying Abbie, and greeted Jason with a kiss.

"Gabe told us you didn't find her. Adam isn't back yet. Maybe he had better luck,"

Jason reached for the baby. "Let me hold Abbie. I need to remind myself she's safe. I don't know what I'd do if I were in Karen's shoes."

"That makes two of us," replied Rachel.

Karen looked around the room at her new family. She was very glad to have them to keep her company.

Larry came into the kitchen.

"Mama, can I have some milk and cookies?"

Karen lifted a brow.

"What do you say?"

"Please, may I have some milk and cookies?"

Karen ruffled his hair. "Yes, you may. Would you like to eat in here or take it to the living room?"

"The living room, please. I figure I'll see Patty first when she gets home."

Happy to perform this normal task in such a crazy, horrible day, she got the food, carried it to the living room and set it on the coffee table.

Larry followed.

She opened her arms. "Give me a hug, son."

He wrapped his arms around her waist.

"You're a good big brother, you know that, don't you?"

He buried his face in her stomach and shook his head.

"I didn't stop the lady from taking Patty. I'm not a good brother."

Her chest tightened hearing his distress. "You couldn't help that. The woman was much bigger and stronger than you. She hit Alice with a shovel and she would have hit you, too. I'm very glad she didn't. You acted correctly. I wouldn't want you to have done anything differently. Okay?"

He nodded.

She heard his sob and hugged him tighter.

"I love you, Larry. You and Patty are all that matter to me. Do you understand?"

"Uh huh."

"Good. Now you sit here and enjoy your treat and then we'll get you ready for bed. Okay?"

He leaned his head back and looked at her.

"I love you, too, Mama."

"I know you do."

She released him, bent down, and then kissed his head.

"Go on now. Eat."

He knelt on the floor and picked up a sugar cookie.

Karen watched him for a moment, let the tears clear from her eyes, and then went back to the kitchen.

When she entered the conversation stopped.

"Is he all right?" asked Rachel.

Karen nodded. "He'll be fine. He's blaming himself for Patty being taken. I had to explain that it was not his fault. He's eating his snack, and then I'll put him to bed. You know you all don't have to stay. Adam will be home soon. I'll wait until then. You go on home."

"We don't mind staying." Jason glanced around at the group. "You should have someone with you tonight."

She shook her head. "I have my son. He's all I need right now."

"Very well." Jason took Abbie to her mother. "But send someone for us if you need to. We'll be here quickly."

"Thank you so much for all you've done."

Jason walked over and embraced her. "We'll all go out again tomorrow with the sun. We'll go east this time and find Adam and Patty. I'm sure of it. Try and get some rest."

She hugged him back, needing the strength he gave her. "I will, though I doubt I can sleep. Not until she's in my arms again."

"I understand. But try, anyway."

Once they left, the house was quiet. She almost wished she hadn't sent them away, but she needed to be alone with her son. Larry needed her as much as she needed him.

She put Larry to bed, read him a story and he was asleep before she finished it. Oh, the sleep of children. At times she wished she could rest so easily.

Karen hugged herself around the middle, steps dragging, she went back to the kitchen and poured herself a cup of coffee. Tonight wouldn't be one of the nights she could sleep anyway.

"Oh, Adam," she said aloud. "Where are you? Do you have Patty yet? Please, God let it be so."

Adam rode as fast as he could through the trees. Luckily, he knew where he was headed. Anna didn't and she was on foot with a child. Because of that knowledge, even though she had a two-hour head start, he'd reach the slide before them and stop her before she tried to cross it and got both herself and Patty killed.

The rock slide had been present as long as he could remember and was difficult to cross safely. The rocks perched precariously on one another. One misstep could send a person falling with more rocks falling on top of them.

He reached the slide and dismounted in the trees, hiding his horse in a particularly dense maple grove. He stayed behind one tree, watching the path made by animals. The path was the easiest way to get to the slide.

Adam was soon rewarded for his efforts. Although it was dark, the appearance of Anna with a lantern in one hand and holding Patty with the other meant she carried no satchel or duffle but intended to go forward as quickly as possible. She should have stopped and made a camp, but Adam was glad she hadn't.

When she was about ten feet past him, he stepped out onto the path.

"That's far enough, Anna."

She turned quickly and put the child between them.

"Go away and leave us alone."

"That won't happen. I'm taking Patty home to her mother."

"I'm her mother now."

"Adam," shouted Patty, shaking her hand loose from Anna's, she started to run to him.

Anna grabbed her by the hair and yanked her back.

Patty screamed and fell to the ground.

Adam had seen enough. He ran to Patty, and as he approached, Anna pulled Patty by the hair toward the slide.

"Let her go, you bitch. Or you'll deal with me."

Anna let go of Patty, turned and ran for the slide.

He didn't care what she did as long as she let Patty go. Adam picked up the little girl, his daughter, and held her close until her sobs quieted.

"Come on, sweetheart. Let's go home."

He walked back to his horse and mounted. Then leaned down and lifted Patty onto his lap.

Her whole body shook and she burrowed into him, hiding herself.

He wrapped one arm around her and held the reins with the other.

"You're safe now Patty. You'll be in Mama's arms soon."

Adam rode as quickly as possible in the receding daylight. He didn't want to have to stop and make a camp.

They reached Seattle after nine.

Patty had fallen asleep in his arms. Her face nuzzled into his chest, unwilling even in slumber to break the connection.

He dismounted, with some difficulty, while holding Patty. Adam wrapped the reins around the hitching rail in front of Karen's house and then walked up the path to the porch. No sooner had he placed his foot on the bottom step, when Karen opened the door and flew to him.

"You found her. Thank you. Thank you for bringing my baby home."

She held out her arms.

Adam placed the little girl in her mother's arms.

Karen held her close. Kissing her face, her hair, raising her hand and kissing it, too.

"How can I ever thank you."

Adam smiled at the sight of mother and daughter.

"She's my daughter now, too. Let's go inside. I could use something to eat and so could she. I know she's sleeping, but I doubt she's eaten much since Anna took her. Anna wasn't carrying anything that I could see that would hold food or anything else."

Karen turned and went inside to the kitchen.

Adam followed. He removed his hat and ran a hand through his hair.

She looked between the child she held and the stove. Then she returned Patty to Adam. "Will you hold her while I prepare your dinners?"

"With pleasure."

"What happened with Anna?"

Adam frowned as he settled into a kitchen chair with Patty on his lap. "I left her. I was too anxious to bring Patty back to you and I just didn't care what happened to Anna."

Karen put a hand to her throat. "But, what if she comes back?"

I should have brought her along, but I was in too much of a hurry to walk all the way back here, while Anna and Patty rode my horse. So, what did happen to Anna? Did she die? Cross the slide? Or will she darken our doorstep again?

Moments later, Patty refused to sit in a chair to eat, preferring to sit in Adam's lap. She wouldn't leave his side.

Whenever Adam stood, whether to get more food or take his dishes to the sink, Patty followed him.

At bedtime, she insisted that Adam tuck her in and read her a story.

Adam looked to Karen and shrugged. "What should I do?"

"She's still scared, and you rescued her. She feels safe with you. Go ahead and indulge her for a day or two. By then, she'll be back to wanting me…I hope."

"Karen, she's just a baby. Don't take any of this to heart."

Karen shook her head and waved him off.

"Don't worry. I understand how she feels. You brought my baby back to me. I feel safe with you and trust you to find Anna and see that she is arrested."

He brushed his knuckle slowly down her cheek. Relief washed through him. *She's forgiven me.* "I will I promise."

Chapter 11

Crouched behind a bush off the path, Anna Jacobsen watched the man ride away with her child. Karen Martell owed her a child and the girl was the one she chose. She was about the age her son would have been if Karen had done her job. His death was her fault. Hers. And she would pay.

If her husband hadn't kept her locked up, she'd have paid Karen back before now. But by the time her husband had her released from the asylum, Karen had left New Bedford. Her husband was no help, he told her he'd send her away again if she didn't stop ranting about Karen Martell. So she never mentioned her to him again.

Instead she found out where Karen went by talking to Karen's former neighbors who were more than happy to spread the story of how she became a mail-order bride. Anna sold every piece of jewelry her husband ever gave her to get passage to Seattle. She had nothing left.

She'd been living off of garbage heaps and whatever she could steal. The garbage behind the Seattle Inn was especially good. All the food left on the plates of the diners was thrown into a can in the back. It was like a slop bucket for pigs. They burned the trash once a week but until then the food was plentiful.

But now, eating wasn't foremost in her mind. If she couldn't have the child she wanted, then maybe the time had come to get rid of the mother. Then she'd take both children. They'd be hers. If she had the children, her husband would take her back. All she had to do was kill Karen Martell.

She didn't have a gun. Wouldn't know how to use the weapon if she had one.

Anna watched the man who took her new daughter, until he was out of sight and then followed him as quickly and quietly as she could. She needed to find shelter. The oil in the lantern she'd stolen wouldn't last forever. If she could make it back to the cabin with the old man, she'd be safe. He'd let her stay; after all, she'd vacated the cabin. He owed her.

She trudged along the path back the way she'd come. Why hadn't the man made her go with them? Did he leave her on purpose, hoping she'd die in the wilderness? If that was his plan, it was a bad one. She wouldn't die. Not today. Definitely, not today.

Karen went with Adam when he put Patty to bed.

They returned to the kitchen. She folded her hands on the table in front of her. "Thank you for bringing her back. But I want you to know that this doesn't change what is between us. I don't intend to let you into my bed, other than to sleep…yet."

Adam sighed. "I understand, but I'd hoped your gratitude would extend to us making love."

She shook her head. "It wouldn't be making love. You don't love me. It would be having relations and I want more than that."

He raised an eyebrow. "You said except for sleep. So I am to share your bed after all."

"Only because the children, especially now, need to see that their parents care for each other and get used to you sleeping with me. They still come to my room when they're scared. They need to stop doing that."

Adam reached over and placed his hand on top of hers. "No. When they are frightened, they should come to you…us. They need to know we're there and they're safe."

She smiled. "You really do know about children. I think you'll make a wonderful father."

"You forget I had practice with Billy."

"You're right I forgot. All of you raised Billy together."

"That's right, we did."

"I suppose we should go to bed now."

"We should." But he remained seated.

She stood and looked around the kitchen to make sure everything was tidy and to avoid looking at him. "I'll undress first like last night. You can come in later."

He nodded. "All right, but I promise I won't look. I wouldn't humiliate you that way. Someday, soon I hope, you'll be excited for me to see you undress and you won't be embarrassed when I do."

Karen gathered their coffee cups and took them to the sink. "You didn't bring much in the way of clothing with you. Just that one small valise."

"I have a change of clothes. That'll do."

She spun around to face him. "But…but you didn't bring anything to sleep in. Where are your pajamas?"

He grinned. "Don't wear them. I sleep in the nude. I did last night and you didn't say anything."

Her eyes widened and her mouth fell open. "Not here, you don't. I have children and you need to be clothed. What if one or both of them climb into bed with us? And I didn't watch you last night. How would I know what you slept in or…not?"

He lifted an eyebrow. "They'll have to learn when our door is shut, they can't come in."

Lord, just the thought of his nude body next to me in bed makes me hot. I feel like I need to fan myself, but I can't have him naked, as much as I want to. The kids come first. "What if, as you said, they're scared? Kids get scared, remember?"

He shrugged. "Then you'll have to make sure they climb in on your side or that they don't get under the sheet."

"Wouldn't wearing pajamas be easier?"

"Easier on your sensibilities, you mean." He stood, started toward her, then stopped. "What are you afraid of, Karen? I won't hurt you. You've already had children so coupling should give you no pain."

She took a deep breath. *Why can't he understand?* "It's not the pain I fear. I want your respect. You don't respect me if you believe I would seduce young Ethan. Or that I might try to influence Jason with my feminine wiles."

Adam put his hands in his pockets. "I do respect you. More than any woman I know, for the most part. I think you're amazing. Raising the children on your own and working as a doctor, and a darn good one at that." He walked to where she leaned against the sink, and placed his hands on her shoulders. "Look. I made a mistake. I'm sorry. I really am."

Karen shook off his hands and walked around him. She needed space. When his hands were on her and he stood so close, she could smell his scent,

141

a wonderful combination of sandalwood, pine trees and man. She could lose herself in that scent. And she couldn't afford to do that, not now…not yet.

"We need to start over, Adam. Just because we're married doesn't mean you don't have to court me, or that we don't have to get to know each other before we have relations. I want the courtship, the flowers and candy and moonlight walks, picnics with the kids. All of those things that go along with a courtship."

She turned away from him. "I'm going to bed. You can sleep in your drawers tonight." Rounding on him, she put up one finger and shook it at him. "But tomorrow you will get pajamas."

He grinned even wider than before. "I don't wear drawers."

Again, her mouth fell open. She shut it and looked heavenward. "Give me strength enough to deal with this infernal, aggravating man."

Adam laughed.

The man would be the death of her. She walked away into the bedroom.

He followed her, chuckling the whole way.

"Which side of the bed do you sleep on?"

She pointed toward the wall. "That side. Douglas always slept on the side toward the door. He said that was so he could protect me from pirates, should we be attacked." The memory made her smile. Even if she was thinking about her dead husband, he loved to see her smile.

He told himself he shouldn't rile her, but she was so responsive...so passionate. He wanted that passion. Wanted to see her eyes glaze over in pleasure when they made love. They may not actually love each other, but the phrase sounded so much better than having relations.

He'd tried love once and that was enough for him. Adam couldn't go through that kind of pain again.

But she can't leave you at the altar, like Phoebe and Ralph. She's already your wife.

That much was true, but that wouldn't stop her from leaving him for another man. A rich man, or at least richer than Adam. That was the reason Phoebe left him. Money. She had professed to love him, so she couldn't have loved Frank.

None of those issues mattered anymore. Those memories, that circumstance could never happen again, so why couldn't he leave them there...in the past...where they belonged?

He rubbed his hands over his face, to rub the memories away.

"Adam? Is something wrong? You're just staring off into space and haven't heard a thing I said, have you?"

He sighed and slowly blinked his eyes, which felt dry all of a sudden. "You're right. I was thinking about something else."

"Can I help? Whatever it was seems to vex you."

She'd tilted her head and gazed at him with those big blue eyes of hers. Standing next to the bed, she held a pink gown in one hand.

"No. Thank you, but it's a problem I need to solve on my own."

"As you wish. Will you please turn around so I can put on my nightgown?"

"Of course." He walked over to her, took her hand and brought it to his lips. "Forgive me for my oafish behavior a bit ago. Making love is no trivial matter, and I need to show you the respect you deserve. You're right about that."

Her blush made him feel worse for upsetting her before.

Adam turned his back and let her undress and get under the covers before he turned around.

"If you'll blow out the lamp, I'll undress and get into bed."

She blew it out. "Thank you, for understanding."

"I should have been a better husband and not argued or tried to embarrass you. You're right. We should know each other better and please know that I won't force you...ever."

"I'm glad to hear that. I wasn't sure after the incident at Jason's."

"I know and I just wanted to reassure you, you're safe with me."

Moonlight streamed in the window enough to see her.

She nodded, but didn't say more.

He climbed into the bed, on top of the sheet, in respect for her sensibilities and careful to stay on his side.

They lay there quiet for a few minutes. The only sounds were their breathing and the crickets outside the window.

"Adam."

"Yes."

"You know the one thing I miss most about Douglas?"

He tensed, expecting to hear some secret that he couldn't accomplish.

"What?"

She turned toward him. "I miss cuddling in bed. I think that's why I started letting the children sleep with me."

He raised his arm so it was straight above her.

"Come here."

She scooted next to him and he enveloped her with his arm.

Karen laid her head on his arm and placed her arm on his stomach and chest.

"This is nice. Thank you."

"Anytime. Now go to sleep. You need your rest."

Sleep was a long time coming for him. He couldn't stop sniffing her head and the scent of violets she wore. He liked it. Most women wore lilac or rose water as their perfume of choice. Not

Karen. His Karen was unique even down to her cologne water.

He closed his eyes and wondered what morning would bring. Anna wasn't done with them. He was sure of it.

He awakened to someone pounding on the front door and knew he wasn't wrong about Anna. Karen opened her eyes, terror shining in them.

"What is that?"

"I'll go see. Turn your head. I still don't have any clothes on."

She turned toward the wall.

After he'd donned his pants, he grabbed his shirt off the peg.

"You can look now."

He watched her, saw her eyes widen and her luscious mouth form a silent "O", making him want more than anything to kiss her until she begged him to take her. But he wanted more than just her body. He wanted her heart. Wanted her to forget her first husband and think only of him, not just when they made love but always.

"I'll be right back, as soon as I find out who is pounding on our door.

She nodded and swallowed.

He had an effect on her, a positive effect. This was good, oh yes, very good.

She then threw back the covers. "I need to check on the kids."

He nodded and put his beautiful bride out of his mind, he put on his holster and walked to the front door and pulled it open. Nailed into the wood was another note.

He cursed and plucked it from a nail.

You think you got rid of me, but I'm here and I'll get what I want. You should have killed me when you had the chance.

Adam saw the note was written in pencil and on what looked like note paper from one of the brides. How was she getting into the dormitory? Or was she getting the supplies from the two buildings that were empty? Had the brides left something behind when they consolidated living into just two dormitories? The hammer and nails, she could have gotten from an abandoned cabin, the same with the shovel. Perhaps even the cabin where he found Seth. Regardless of where she found the items, she seemed to be very resourceful.

He would have crumpled the note, but Karen had to see the paper herself. She had to prepare. He'd hire men to keep an eye on the children, and he had men watching the house. Wait. Where was Abe? He was supposed to be on duty now.

Adam pocketed the note, pulled his weapon and walked around the house looking for Abe. Perhaps he'd had to relieve himself. Before Adam had made the trip to the outhouse, he saw Abe, sitting on the ground, legs out in front of him.

He hurried over to him. "Abe? What happened?"

The dark haired man rubbed the back of his head. When he removed his hand, Adam saw blood covering his fingers. Head wounds usually bleed a lot and Abe didn't have much blood on his hand, so the wound didn't appear to be too bad.

"I don't rightly know. One minute I'm patrolling the outside of the house and the next I'm lying here with a goose egg on my head. Someone knocked me out, Boss. I'm sorry. I don't know how the person got behind me."

"She's good at getting around people. Don't worry about it for now."

Abe slowly shook his head. "I can't believe she sneaked up on me. I'm usually more aware than that."

"It doesn't matter. She's very good at sneaking around and not being seen."

"What do you want me to do, Boss? Keep watching the house like I have? If she can get around me I can't see much point in me being here."

Adam chewed on his lower lip for a moment, like he did when he was a boy. "We'll keep doing what we're doing. She'll make a mistake and then she's ours. If by chance you do see her, try and capture her. Or if that doesn't appear possible, see if you can follow her. We need to find out where she's hiding."

Abe rubbed his head. "Sure thing. I owe her for this goose egg she gave me."

Adam nodded. "Yes, you do. We owe her for so much more. If you can apprehend her, I'd be very grateful."

He went inside and found Karen sitting at the kitchen table in her wrapper, staring into her coffee cup. As he entered she looked up.

"Well? The pounding on the door was her, wasn't it?"

Adam nodded. "She left us this." He handed the note to her.

Karen read it and then tossed it on the table. She stood, paced to the sink and looked outside. "The woman is unhinged. Completely insane."

"Agreed. We'll simply have to be more vigilant. I thought about having more men watch the children separately, but I want them to stay here with you. Quinn will still be here, and I'll put an additional man outside with Abe. I won't let this happen again."

He stopped Karen as she paced between the table and the sink.

"You should probably have a look at Abe's head. She knocked him out and cut his scalp, but I don't think it was too bad. We'll get her. I won't let her terrorize you."

"A little too late for that. I'll get dressed and check Abe. The wound should be cleaned if nothing else."

This is my fault. I never should have let her go. "I should have brought her back with Patty. None of this would have happened, if I had. I need to talk to the sheriff and see if he's got any leads."

She laid a hand on his arm. "Please, don't blame yourself. You brought my daughter back and that matters more than anything. I'm not worried. I know you'll keep us safe."

He covered her hand with his. "I'll do my very best. I don't want anything to happen to you or the children."

"I know."

Karen went back to the bedroom and dressed, as she returned, a knock sounded from the front door.

They went together to answer it.

Abe stood there with a very distraught man.

"What's the matter?" asked Adam, his arm around Karen's shoulders.

The man, about the same height as Karen and wearing brown pants and a plaid shirt, spoke quickly. "I'm Paul Petersen and it's my wife. She's having our baby. Please Mrs. Martell...er Mrs. Talbot, she needs your help. She's in so much pain."

"I'll be right there." She looked up at Abe. "Would you come in and stay with the children?"

"Yes, ma'am. They'll be safe with me."

"Thank you." She turned to Adam. "I'll get my bag."

"I'll be here."

A few minutes later Karen returned with her Gladstone bag in hand.

"I'm ready." She addressed Mr. Petersen. "Do you have a wagon or do we walk?"

"We have to walk, I'm afraid," said Mr. Petersen. "I can't afford a wagon and our cabin is about two miles outside of town."

"My horse and Abe's are tied out front." Adam looked at Karen. "You'll ride with me. Abe will stay inside with the children, and Mr. Petersen will ride Abe's horse."

"That'd be great," said Mr. Petersen.

Karen talked to Abe before heading out the door. "Please take the children to Dormitory One and ask for Alice. She'll see that you all have breakfast."

Adam took Karen's bag.

"All right Mr. Petersen, we'll follow you."

The man practically ran down the path from the porch to the hitching rails where the horses were tied.

He stopped at the end of the rail and looked back at Adam.

"Which one do I ride?"

"The bay mare." Adam pointed at the reddish-brown horse.

Adam's horse was solid black and magnificent. He was proud of Midnight every time he rode him.

The saddles lay hanging on the rail. As long as Abe was guarding the house, Adam didn't worry about theft. Besides, Midnight would stand out like a sore thumb. Everyone in Seattle was aware who the horse belonged to and wouldn't dare steal it. Adam and Abe made quick work of saddling their horses.

Adam helped Karen to mount, handed her the Gladstone bag and then mounted behind her.

By the time they did that, Petersen was on top of the bay and pulling away, headed out of town toward Tacoma.

They rode for a good quarter-hour into the woods before a small cabin, sitting in a clearing, came into view.

Mr. Petersen jumped off his horse, practically before the animal stopped and ran into the structure.

Adam and Karen followed.

On either side of the door were neat flower beds full of green plants that had yet to bloom. The path to the house was paved with flat stones. Mrs. Peterson obviously took great pride in her little log cabin.

The door slammed shut.

Startled, Karen swung around.

Grinning at her was Anna Jacobsen, holding a rifle, pointed directly at Karen.

CHAPTER 12

"Well, I'm so glad you all could join us," she sneered. "I've waited too long for this moment."

In the bed on the side of the cabin to the right of the door, Karen saw a woman in obvious heavy labor.

She started toward her.

Anna pointed the rifle at Karen. "Stop right there, Mrs. Martell."

Karen stiffened her spine and, with narrowed eyes, turned to Anna. "I'm helping this woman. If you want to shoot me, go ahead."

Anna thought a moment, glared at her, then took the rifle and pointed to Mrs. Petersen. "Go on. I'll shoot you after you deliver her baby. And everything better be right. I won't let you kill her child, like you did mine."

"I didn't kill your baby and you know it." Karen went to Mrs. Petersen. "I know the pain hurts, but soon you'll have a beautiful baby to hold in your arms. Now tell me how long you've been in labor."

"Since about midnight," said Mr. Petersen, as he took his wife's hand. "I'm sorry about the woman. She took my rifle when I was out chopping wood. I didn't know it. Genny's labor had started. That's when she," he jutted his head toward Anna. "Came in holding my gun on us. She waited here for hours, until Genny's labor pains were comin' on quicker. Then, that woman made me go get you. Said she'd kill Genny if I said anything to you. I couldn't risk that."

"Of course, you couldn't," said Adam. "I'd have done the same thing. My wife is too precious to me."

Karen glanced over at Adam lifted an eyebrow, before turning back to Genny. "Is Genny short for something, dear?" asked Karen.

"Genevieve," said the woman between pains. "But call me Genny."

"All right, Genny. I need you to raise your knees so I can see what's happening."

Genny raised her knees and let them fall open.

Karen pulled a sheet over her legs to protect her modesty.

"Mr. Petersen, please put some water on the stove to heat."

Mr. Petersen hurried to do Karen's bidding. There was already a bucket on the stove and he opened the burner, tossed in some kindling, making the fire burn hotter. Then he walked to the bed and kissed his wife.

"You're doing great, love." He turned.

She stopped him. "Don't leave me, Paul."

He glanced over at Karen.

She nodded. "Let her hold your hands. It will help her through the pain."

Mr. Petersen took his wife's hands and smiled at her. "We'll do this together."

"Adam, please bring me that lamp." She pointed at the one on the table next to where Anna stood.

Adam ignored Anna and plucked the lamp off the table.

"Here you go," he said, careful to avert his gaze.

Karen took the lamp and then turned to Anna. "As you are the only other woman here, I need you to hold the lamp for me."

Anna hesitated, and then she looked at Adam. "If you come near me or try to take this gun, I'll bash Karen over the head with the lamp. As a matter of fact, you go over there." She used the gun and pointed at the kitchen. "Stay there, understand?"

Adam nodded and walked to the kitchen.

Anna walked over to the bed and then lowered the gun. She took the light from Karen and held it so she could see.

"Well, everything looks all right down here. Your baby is just beginning to crown so I want you to push. Push with all your might."

Genny pushed and the head came a little farther out.

"Push again. Harder. Come on you can do it," encouraged Karen.

Pushing, resting, pushing, resting. Genny did it over and over until the head was clear.

Karen smiled at the tired woman. "Okay, that was the hard part. Now I want you to push again. Bear down with all your might. Take a breath and push."

Genny did as asked and soon the baby slid from her into Karen's waiting hands.

"There you go. You can rest now. I'll get this little one cleaned up, and you'll hold her in just a minute or two."

"Her," said Genny. "You said her."

"Yes." Karen smiled. She reached in her bag for scissors, tied off the umbilical cord and then cut it. "You have a beautiful baby girl." She turned toward Anna. "You can lower the lamp now. Thank you, Anna"

The woman took the lamp back to the table, but Karen saw the tears in her eyes.

"I had a son," whispered Anna. "He was born dead. I've never seen a birth before. Giving birth is hard. I know what birthing a babe feels like, but I've never seen it. It's a miracle."

"Yes, it is." Karen looked up at Mr. Petersen where he stood by the headboard, holding his wife's hand. She never tired of seeing beaming, happy parents. "Mr. Petersen, do you have a basin to put the warm water in? I need to clean up your daughter. Do you have a name picked out?"

"We're calling her Grace," he responded without ever looking away from his weary wife.

"That's lovely. The water now please. No more than two inches in the basin and I'll need a washcloth."

"Oh, yes."

He hurried to the stove and poured water into a battered metal bowl. Then he checked the temperature with his finger and added a little cold water. From a shelf over the counter he grabbed the washrag.

Karen took the baby to the table and waited for the father with the basin. When he set it down, she tested it herself and, finding it just warm, set the baby in it and using the washcloth, cleaned all the birthing material off of her, despite the little one's fussing. She was pink all over and waving her arms, protesting Karen's ministrations.

"I have a special blanket for her," said Genny. "It's here next to me."

Anna laid the rifle on the floor and, without being asked, retrieved the blanket and handed it to Karen.

She took the little quilt, laid it on the table and wrapped the wet baby inside it, drying her as she wrapped. Karen didn't swaddle the child too tight.

She knew the parents would remove the blanket anyway to count toes and fingers and touch the wispy hair on her head.

Grace was very blonde, like both her parents and like most babies she had blue eyes. The color could change or it might remain blue.

Karen picked up her bag with all manner of supplies that, thankfully, she hadn't needed.

Adam quietly picked up the gun and aimed it toward Anna. "Time to go. I'm not letting you get away this time."

She looked up, tears still in her eyes. "I won't fight you. Seeing this baby be born brought back so many memories. I remember now the struggle Mrs. Martell went through trying to save my baby. Yes, I still remember the pain, but I also remember her cleaning up my son so I could hold him. She didn't have to do that."

Mr. Petersen came forward and pressed two silver dollars into Karen's hand.

"Thank you. Thank you so much for my daughter."

Karen wasn't blind, she had seen the house when she came in and knew that the Petersen's had very little. She looked down at the money and shook her head. "You keep it."

"No. It is for you. I've been saving just for this."

Adam looked at her.

Karen watched his mouth form a thin line when her hand closed over the money.

"All right." She put the money in the pocket of her skirt. "We should go now and leave this family to get better acquainted."

Adam nodded, his back stiff and his gaze narrowed when he looked at her.

What did she do? Why was he angry?

Karen gazed over at the Petersen's. They looked blissfully happy. "Come get me if you need to. If you can bring her to me it will save time."

"We will. Thank you, Mrs. Talbot."

Petersen looked back down at his family.

If the possibility existed for a man to glow, he was glowing. Karen smiled and joined Adam and Anna outside.

He'd tied Anna to the bay Petersen had ridden out. Now, he waited beside the big black horse for Karen. His face wasn't any friendlier than it had been inside.

She walked to the horse and set her Gladstone bag on the ground. Lifting her leg she put her foot in the stirrup. From there Adam lifted her into the saddle and after tying the bag to the saddle, he climbed up behind her.

He held the reins to their horse in his left hand and those to Anna's horse in his right.

Adam clicked his tongue and touched his heels to the horses flank.

"Giddy up. Let's go."

Karen didn't have Adam's arm around her to steady her on this trip, and so she hung on to the saddle horn with both hands.

After they'd ridden for about ten minutes, she broke the silence.

"Why are you angry? What did I do?"

"Nothing."

"Your anger isn't nothing. *Something* caused it."

"Very well. You took that man's money, even though you know he can't afford it. I thought you were different, that money wasn't your motivation. But, it is. Money. You're just like Phoebe."

Anger rose in her. "You think I'm like your ex-fiancée, who left you for a rich man, just because I let someone pay me for my services? You are such a hypocrite. What would you do if a poor man needed lumber for his home? What if he couldn't pay you? Would you give him the lumber anyway? Of course, you wouldn't. You'd tell the man to come back when he had the money."

She sat stiff as a board in front of him, not wanting their bodies to touch.

"That's not the same."

She turned as much as possible, so she could see him. "You're right it's not the same, because I *give* my services to anyone, whether they pay me or not. I can't walk out on an expectant mother just because she's poor."

"But you took his money, and you know they can't afford it."

He's making me crazy. How can he be so dense and judgmental? "So what? I got paid for my services. I have children to feed, clothe and put a roof over their heads, too."

"I'll take care of that now."

"Oh, really? So you expect me to work for free?"

He closed his mouth and looked away.

"Of course, not."

"Then what are you saying?"

He stared at her, his eyes almost slits. "Well, he was so poor...and..."

"And he said he'd been saving for this event. How do you think he'd have felt if I didn't take his money? He needed to pay me as much for the service I provided, as for his dignity. And if you must know, when I run into people like them, I take their money and buy things as gifts for the baby. They can't turn them down that way."

Adam's shoulders sagged. "Karen, I—"

"Don't talk to me, Adam. Just don't talk." She faced forward, not wanting to see his face. "I know what you think of me now. You told me you respected and admired me, but that isn't true. You think I, like all women, are only after money because you were hurt. Well, get over your anger at Phoebe and see me and the rest of the world without the angry brush you paint us with."

He leaned forward and kissed her hair.

She gasped and moved her head away. "Don't."

He leaned back so he wasn't touching her. "You're right. I'm sorry. I thought I was over Phoebe and Frank's betrayal, but I'm obviously not.

All I can do now is ask for your forgiveness and promise you I'll try to do better."

"Like the last two times?"

He blew out a breath. "I can't take back my words, they were spoken out loud and in anger, but I promise, in the future, I'll think about what I say first."

"I'm not sure there is a future for us. I know we're married, but the marriage can be annulled."

Anna began to laugh. "Trouble in paradise, Mrs. Martell?"

Karen turned to the right and glared at the woman. She was back to her crazy self. But for a moment, she'd been just another mother watching a baby be born and was touched by it. "It's Mrs. Talbot and keep your remarks to yourself."

Adam put the reins for both horses in his right hand, wrapped his left around Karen's waist and gently pulled her back against him.

"Don't call us quits. Please, give me a chance to prove—"

"Prove what? You've already shown your true feelings. You can't take those back. The cat's out of the bag."

She closed her eyes and let herself lean back against him. Keeping her back so stiff, was painful and riding wasn't easy while holding the saddle horn with both hands.

He leaned down and whispered in her ear. "I'm sorry, Karen. Truly I am."

She slowly shook her head. "You're always sorry after the fact. We've got a long road ahead if we're to make this marriage work. If you aren't ready to work then we should get it annulled now and save the anguish that is inevitably ahead of us. I can't trust what you say when your actions are the total opposite of your words." In her anger, Karen's chest tightened, her stomach clenched and she couldn't take a deep breath.

"Can't you forgive me and let us start fresh?"

"I don't honestly know. You'll have to give me some time to think."

"All right. Take the time you need. I'm not going anywhere."

She jutted her chin at Anna. "Let's just take her to Sheriff Kearney. Let him deal with her."

"I'll drop you off first, and then I'll take her to the sheriff. Don't worry, she's not getting away, this time."

They rode to Karen's house. Karen wasn't taking patients today because she'd been out on a delivery and hadn't known when she'd be back.

Adam dismounted, and then tied the horse Anna rode to the hitching rail before lifting Karen to the ground and handing her the Gladstone bag.

"I'll be back as soon as I can.".

She stood, with her back as straight as a broomstick, and stared up at him, doing nothing to hide her anger. "Take your time. I have to gather the children and see that they and Abe are fed lunch. Regardless of what happens between us, my children are always my first priority."

Adam nodded. "As it should be."

She turned and went up the path to the house, carrying her Gladstone bag. *I still love him. But he doesn't respect or trust me. If he gets jealous of every man I come in contact with our relationship...our marriage...will never work. What will I do?*

CHAPTER 13

Adam dropped Anna off with the sheriff, Brand Kearney. Brand placed Anna in one of the two cells in the jail then came out and took Adam's statement.

Brand folded the paper and placed it in an envelope. "I'll file the charges and take her to Olympia for trial."

He was a good man and a good sheriff, so Adam put Anna Jacobsen out of his mind. She was no longer a threat to Karen or the kids.

Then he headed to Karen's house, riding Midnight and leading Abe's horse through town. He wasn't sure he could call her house his home. Their marriage was far from certain and that situation was his fault. He'd treated her like she was Phoebe though Karen was nothing like her. How would he prove to Karen he changed? That he understood and wouldn't make that mistake again.

Suddenly, Adam remembered her grandmother's broken music box. If he fixed it, maybe he would get into Karen's good graces again. Maybe she'd know that he cared.

He tied the horses to the rail and went into the house. Abe was still at the dormitory with the children. The house was empty.

Adam went into the kid's room and found the small, intricately carved wooden music box on a shelf. To keep it safe and hidden, in case Karen came in, he put it under his shirt and hurried out to his horse.

Fred Longmire waved as he rode by on his way to Jason's. Fred was sweeping the boardwalk outside his store.

Adam waved and rode on.

He slipped from Midnight, wrapped the reins around the hitching rail and went inside.

It was lunch time, and Jason and Rachel sat at the kitchen table eating by themselves.

Jason looked up.

"Adam. What are you doing here? Is everything all right? Did that woman come back?"

"Everything is fine. Yes, the woman came back but we caught her and now she's in jail…a threat to no one. Never mind that. I need your help."

Jason put his napkin on the table next to his plate and stood.

"What can I help you with?"

Adam pulled the little music box from his shirt.

"I need to fix this for Karen and I don't have any idea where to start."

"Why don't we ask Ben Bundy? He was a watchmaker before he became a lumberjack."

Adam extended his arm to hand the box to Jason. "That would be great. Can you talk to him as soon as possible?"

Jason shook his head and waved his hand. "Why don't *you* talk to him? After all you are the one who needs it repaired."

Adam ran a hand through his hair. "Of course, you're right. I don't know what I was thinking. Karen has got me questioning everything I do. I've misjudged her badly, and I—"

Rachel stood and joined the men. "I'm sure you haven't done anything so awful that she won't forgive you. She cares for you greatly."

"And I her," admitted Adam. His chest warmed and his pulse beat faster with the confession.

His sister-in-law put her hand on his arm.

"Have you told her? That you care?"

"No. Instead, I keep acting like she's Phoebe."

"Ah," said Rachel. "I see. What happened between you and Phoebe has you not trusting women. But Karen isn't any woman. She's your wife."

"That's why I want to fix the music box. I want to show her I care about her and the kids. Those kids are great. Patty doesn't want to leave my side since I brought her home. I don't think Patty's new obsession with me pleases her mother very much. Sorry. I'm rambling." Adam's shoulders sagged. "I hate to see Karen unhappy."

Rachel squeezed his arm. "She'll get over it. Just do whatever you have to do to help Patty through this trauma. Karen will do the same. And, by the way, I think it's wonderful you want to fix her grandmother's music box. That little box means a great deal to her. It is the only thing she has to remember her grandmother by."

"I saw the tears in her eyes when she discovered it wouldn't work. I think I'll go find Ben Bundy. The sooner he gets this done, the sooner I might get in my wife's good graces."

Jason laughed. "You need more help than that. You've made several mistakes with Karen, that I know about and you have a lot to make up for."

Adam sighed and ran a hand behind his neck. The gesture was one all of the brothers did when frustrated and when he realized what he was doing…he stopped and put his hand in his pocket.

He poured himself some coffee and sat at the table with his hands around the cup. "What can I do to convince her that I've learned and that I really do respect her? I think she's amazing but, as she says I've used whatever distrustful brush I learned to use after Phoebe and painted Karen."

Rachel sat across from Adam. "Have you explained what happened with Phoebe? Perhaps doing that would help her to understand you."

"Some." *I hate thinking about the incident much less talking about it.* "She knows something happened with her but she doesn't know the complete details."

Jason sat in his normal chair at the head of the table. "Maybe it's time you told her, brother. Your outbursts are easier to understand if your background is known."

"Might as well. I can't bungle it any worse than I have." He stood. "Thanks for your help and your advice. I'll think about what you've said but, for now, I'll find Ben and see if he can repair this." He held up the music box and then walked out of the kitchen.

What will I do if Ben can't repair this box? Even if he can, what if Karen still won't forgive me?

Ben Bundy wasn't hard to find. It was his turn to cook for the crews since the Talbots had not hired a permanent cook. Also he was hard to miss since he was about six foot, five inches with flaming red hair and a full, well-maintained beard that went down to his chest.

Adam walked into the long building that served as the cookhouse. Inside on the far end was a kitchen with two, four burner stoves, a huge four door icebox, counter with cupboards above and below, and five rows of tables which seated one hundred men at a time.

He went up to Ben as he stood stirring a pot on one of the stoves. "Hi, Ben. Sorry to bother you, but I need your help."

Ben continued to stir a pot of stew.

"What can I help you with, Adam?"

Adam showed him the small music box. "It quit working, and I need to know if you can fix it. You're the only person we know of that has any experience with this kind of delicate workings. You were a watchmaker, right?"

"Sure was. Would have continued, but there just wasn't enough money in watch making to support a family. So I came here and not only found a job but a bride, too."

"Congratulations. Who is your bride to be?"

"Miss Martha Haller. She's just a little thing with brown hair and eyes and the nicest smile. She's a bit bucktoothed but cute as a button to me. Now let me see that box."

He held out a hand.

Adam gave the box to him.

Ben opened the music box and looked at the workings.

"This should be easy to fix. I see a broken wheel. Once I replace that, the music should play again."

Adam let out the breath he'd been holding. "Thank you. When do you think you'll have it ready?"

Ben lifted an eyebrow. "Well, now, if you stir this stew and the pot of beans and watch the biscuits in the oven, I'll have it back to you in about half an hour. Otherwise not until tomorrow."

Adam smiled. "I'll be glad to watch your food. I'm a cook myself, so I shouldn't have any problem."

"Good. I'll return in a bit. Oh, if anyone comes early, tell them they have to wait just like everyone else."

Adam stepped up to the stove, raised the lid on the pot of beans and looked inside. "I've done this before. You just go fix that thing for me. I'll owe you a favor."

"I'll keep that in mind."

Ben turned and left the building.

Adam thanked his lucky stars for Ben Bundy because after seeing the workings inside the music box, he knew he couldn't have repaired it.

About thirty minutes after he left, Ben returned grinning.

"There you go, Adam. Good as new." Ben put a hand in his pocket and rocked back on his heels. "Now about that favor you owe me."

Adam pulled two large pans of biscuits from the oven, set them on the counter to cool and put two more pans into the oven. "Sure, what do you need?"

"Martha wants a church wedding and needs someone to walk her down the aisle. Since her father isn't here, would you do that for her?"

Adam clapped Ben on the shoulder. "I'd be more than happy to give Martha away. Just let me know when."

"This Saturday at ten o'clock. Be there at a quarter 'til."

"Will do. See you then."

Adam turned and headed home. He couldn't wait to show this to Karen. Surely, she'd forgive him when she saw the repaired music box. Wouldn't she?

Karen had just finished with her last patient, one of the brides who was expecting. She thought she heard two heart beats but couldn't be sure. Based on what she heard through her stethoscope one baby may have been behind the other and so differentiating between the two sounds was difficult. She would keep these thoughts to herself, until she was sure.

She showed the woman out and was surprised to see the only person in the living room was Adam.

He stood by the sofa with his hands behind his back and a grin on his face.

Karen walked over to him. "What are you so happy about? I thought you were working."

"This occasion was more important."

"What?"

He brought his hand forward.

She saw he held her music box.

"What are you doing with that? It's broken."

"Not anymore."

He lifted the lid on the small wooden box. Music poured forth and Karen's mouth fell open.

"But how? I never saw you take it."

"I grabbed it this morning. I figured you wouldn't miss it until tonight. Do you want it?"

She reached for the treasure, amazed at the thoughtfulness of his gesture. "Thank you. You don't know how much this means to me." *This is my first courting gift.*

"I guessed it was pretty precious, because you had tears in your eyes when you told me it didn't work."

She brushed away a tear. "It appears I have tears again now. But I will not cry. I can't have red rimmed eyes when I greet my next patient." She looked around the room. "I don't understand why there is no one here."

"I put out a sign that you were closed between noon and one o'clock for lunch. That way, you can go have the meal with your kids or stay here and let me cook for you."

She was delighted with his action. The break would allow her to rest as well as eat. "You can't be cooking for me every day. You have to work, don't you?"

"Yes, but I set my own hours, so if I want to have lunch with my wife, I will."

Karen smiled. "I don't understand you, Adam Talbot."

He stepped forward and wrapped his arms around her.

She didn't object. She wanted him to hold her more than anything but the situation between them hadn't been settled yet. Still, she stood, taking in his scent, sandalwood and pine and feeling the strength in his embrace. He'd taken the time and made the effort to please her by repairing her grandmother's precious gift, and she was pleased.

"I'm a simple man with simple needs. I'm not afraid to admit I need you. I want this marriage to work, and I'll do whatever I have to for that to happen. If that means we wait to consummate our vows, so be it."

Karen looked up into sincere blue eyes. Was she wrong? He only seemed to have her and the children's best interests at heart.

He took an arm from around her and gently tweaked her nose with his fingers.

"You're thinking too hard. We need a diversion and one of the brides, Martha Haller, has asked me to walk her down the aisle on Saturday. Will you and the kids go with me?"

"Of course, we'll go." She grinned and her heart felt lighter. "I'm so glad Martha found someone. Have you met her fiancé, Ben Bundy?"

He nodded. "He works for us. Did you know he used to be a watchmaker? He also is the one who repaired your music box." His eyebrows bunched together and his expression turned serious. "I didn't know how and was afraid I'd ruin it if I tried, but I had to do something."

"Why?"

"Because the box was from your grandmother and meant so much to you."

"That was very nice of you." She lifted onto her toes and kissed his cheek.

"I'd rather have a real kiss."

He closed the distance between their lips until he was just a whisper away.

"Like this."

Adam didn't mash her lips with his. Instead the kiss started soft. A gentle meeting of mouths. Then he pressed his tongue against her lips, and she opened.

Karen loved his kisses. They always made her feel things that she hadn't in so very long, maybe ever. Douglas never made her body react like Adam could. The center of her being heated and pooled in her lady parts.

She wanted to get closer to him and wrapped her arms around his neck.

He pulled her flush against his body. So close she felt his heart beat, or was that just her own, pounding like a drum against her chest.

Adam pulled back, just a bit.

"I want you," he whispered, his lips grazing hers with his words.

"I want you, too." She'd debated telling him, speaking the words out loud, but she couldn't help it. Her body could only ache for him for so long. "Tonight."

Chapter 14

Karen had barely been able to keep her mind on her patients all afternoon. Excited was the word. She was excited like she'd never been before. Perhaps she was making a mistake, letting Adam make love to her before she was sure he really had changed. That he respected her and knew he had nothing to be jealous about was essential.

But, did he know those things? She hadn't told him she loved him. She wanted him to say the words first. Was that so bad? Maybe. Perhaps he didn't love her, not yet, but she was sure he would, if they gave their marriage a chance.

Making love to him was her giving their marriage a chance. No annulment after tonight. If he wanted to get rid of her he'd have to divorce her.

At supper that night, she could barely eat. Her stomach turned somersaults in anticipation.

Adam gazed at her with eyes smoldering with need.

She suspected hers carried that same look, which disappeared when one of the children said something or needed something. She couldn't wait until they went to bed. Did wanting the kids to go to bed soon make her a bad mother? No, she was just a woman…with needs that hadn't been met in a long time.

The children finished supper and got ready for bed.

"Do you want a story tonight?" Karen asked as she helped them into their pajamas.

"Yes," said Larry.

"From Adam," said Patty.

She ran over, grabbed him around the leg and looked up at him.

"Pease."

Adam looked at Karen and shrugged.

She nodded her head and smiled.

"Guess what else Adam did?" She picked the music box off the shelf. "He fixed Grandmama's music box." She wound it up and let it play while Adam read them their favorite Mother Goose's Nursery Rhyme. They alternated between Mother Goose and Grimm's Fairy Tales.

The music box played on after Adam finished reading and the children had fallen asleep.

Adam closed the book and looked up at Karen from where he sat at the bottom of the bed.

He stood and held out his hand. "Are you ready?"

She nodded and placed her hand in his. "More than ready."

They went to their bedroom and quickly undressed. Karen was a little shy about her body, which showed that she'd had children. Her stretch marks had mostly faded, turning into white lines instead of red or purple. But they were still visible, and she didn't want to turn around, afraid Adam would change his mind about making love.

"Karen. What's the matter, sweetheart?"

"I don't have a young woman's body. I don't want you to be disappointed."

"I didn't marry you for your body. Well that was part of it, I'm very attracted to you physically, but I truly do admire and respect you, more than I ever have any woman. You are absolutely the most interesting woman I've ever met. I don't want a young woman's body. I want yours. No one else's. Yours."

She smiled shyly and turned to face him, forcing her arms to remain at her sides.

He, too, was naked and he was magnificent. She'd seen his chest and arms. Knew how muscular they were, but now seeing all of him, she realized the leashed power behind the beautiful blue eyes.

Adam walked over and cupped her jaw. "You're beautiful. No one can ever be as beautiful to me as you are right now. You're my wife, and we're about to make that a permanent situation. Are you sure?"

She nodded. "I'm sure."

That was all she said. All she needed to say.

He picked her up and carried her to the bed, laying her gently in the middle. He lay beside her, stroking her with a hand while he leaned on the elbow of his other arm.

"You're beautiful."

"I'm glad you think so."

He leaned down and kissed her, touching her only with his lips and the hand that worked up and down her torso, from her breast to her thigh and everything in between.

She reached up, cupped his head with a hand while her other one learned his body, touching everywhere she could reach.

"Adam, I want to feel you inside me. I need you to fill me."

He smiled. "Soon, love, soon."

"No. Now. We can go slow later."

Shaking his head, he grinned. "Why the hurry? But, if it will make you happy, we'll do anything you want, anyway you want." He kissed her lips, her neck, and her breasts, working his way down her body to her center. The one that pooled with need.

His hand caressed her mound and then he pressed one thick finger inside.

"I guess you *are* ready."

Her eyes fell to half-closed. "More than ready. I've been waiting for a long time."

Adam positioned himself over her, kissed her hard and—

Patty opened the door.

"Mama. I don't feel good."

With a groan Adam grabbed the blanket and covered them.

Karen scooted off the bed and put on her robe before going to her daughter.

She picked up the little girl.

"What's the matter, sweetie? Do you hurt anywhere?"

Patty nodded. "Uh huh. My tummy."

"Okay, let's go to the kitchen and see if we can't make you feel better."

Karen turned, looked at Adam and half-smiled. "Interruptions happen when you have children."

He stayed where he was, covered.

"I know. I'll be there after I dress."

Karen was touched that he would get up to see that Patty was all right.

"You don't have to, you know."

He smiled. "I know. But sometimes, kids need their daddy, too."

She nodded. "They do."

In the kitchen, Karen mixed a half spoonful of baking soda in water. She sat Patty on the counter next to the sink and had her drink it.

She took one swallow and pushed the glass away.

"Don't like that."

"I know, baby, but you want your tummy to quit hurting and this will make that happen. You have to drink it down. Come on, now, take another drink."

Patty wrinkled her nose and took another sip. No sooner had she swallowed than she began to throw up into the sink.

When she stopped, she started to cry.

"Oh, honey, don't cry. You feel better now don't you?"

Patty nodded.

"Tummy not hurt."

"Good," said Adam as he walked into the room.

Karen hugged Patty. "She just needed to throw up."

"I saw that." He pointed at the box of baking soda. "I didn't know about using baking soda. That's quite the remedy."

"It soothes stomach upset by getting rid of excess gas or making you throw up. As you can see, my baby needed to get the sick out of her body." She looked at Patty. "Are you ready to go back to bed now?"

The girl shook her head. "I want to sleep with you."

Karen's gaze caught Adam's. He lifted an eyebrow and subtlety shook his head.

She sighed. "Sure, darling, you can sleep with us."

"Karen—"

"I know what you are about to say, but sometimes little ones need the security of sleeping with their mama."

Adam took a deep breath and let it out. "You're right. I'll be sleeping in my pants tonight."

"We should probably get you a pair of pajamas."

He rolled his eyes but nodded. "I suppose so. Tomorrow I'll go see if Fred has any in stock."

Karen tilted her head. "Thank you for understanding."

"Having a little girl is harder than raising a boy. We didn't have to worry about this kind of thing when raising Billy. He had five beds to choose from. We never knew if we'd wake up with him in bed with us or not."

Karen picked up Patty and headed to the bedroom.

"You sleep next to Mama on that side of the bed." She pointed at the side near the wall. "Mama will sleep next to Adam."

Patty shook her head vigorously. "I sleep next to Daddy."

Adam was wide eyed. "Daddy?"

"She's been calling you that since you rescued her. I thought you knew. I think it's sweet."

He shook his head. "No idea, but I like it. Very much."

Karen turned and kissed him. "I thought you might, but I wanted her to say it. I didn't want to tell you, just in case she went back to Adam."

He wrapped his arms around her. "She still might. Billy went through a phase when he called all of us by our first names. He grew out of it when we didn't respond."

Patty stood on the mattress. "I kiss Daddy, too."

Karen laughed. "You can kiss Daddy, too." She moved so Adam could lift Patty in his arms.

"I'd be mighty happy if you'd kiss me right here." He touched his cheek.

She dutifully kissed him.

"And here." He touched the other cheek.

Again, she kissed him.

"And here." He placed a finger on his chin.

Patty laughed, a lovely sound.

"You silly," she said. But she kissed his chin, anyway.

"Okay. You lay down so Mama and Daddy can get in bed and get some sleep."

He set her back on the bed.

She walked to the middle and crawled under the covers.

Karen hastily donned her nightgown and went to the far side of the bed. Adam lay on the near side of the bed with Patty in-between them.

He covered them, blew Karen a kiss, then whispered, "We'll try again tomorrow."

She reached across Patty and cupped his cheek. "You bet we will, and I want you to put a lock on the door, so the kids must knock to come in. That deterrent will give us more time to get dressed. But you still need pajamas or long johns in case one of them needs to sleep with us."

"We should probably teach them not to sleep with us."

"I know, but after Douglas died, I let them because I was lonely in that big bed." *Having them with me was essential to my emotional health. I needed them. Needed to not feel so alone.* "I never really expected to marry again, even though I volunteered to be a mail-order bride. Mostly I simply wanted to start a new life away from all the memories."

"You must have loved him very much."

"I did, but differently than I—" She almost admitted she loved him. Not yet. She wouldn't say it, not yet. Not until she had some indication that he felt the same.

Adam didn't say anything but merely blew out the lamp.

"Goodnight."

"Goodnight."

Sleep was a long time coming. *Did Adam know she was in love with him? She'd almost admitted it. What if he did know and couldn't love her back? What would happen to their marriage then, with love only on one side? Would she begin to resent him?*

Karen awoke to a hand on her breast. At first she thought of Douglas, but then she knew it was Adam who played with her.

"Mmm. That feels nice."

"To me, too."

She knew he kept his voice a mere whisper, lest he wake Patty.

"We should get up. I have to fix breakfast and get the kids to Alice before the patients start arriving."

He took a deep breath and let it out on a sigh, but he didn't remove his hand.

"I suppose we must but I could spend the rest of the day touching you."

She threw off the covers. "And I would let you, but we can't. We have responsibilities."

Groaning, he removed his hand and sat up on the side of the bed.

"I'm moving."

He stood.

She scooted off the bed and all the while Patty slept. Karen looked down at her slumbering child, smiled and then tucked the blankets around her.

Adam put an arm around Karen's shoulders.

"She's such a little thing."

Karen reached up and squeezed his hand as he held her. "She is, and in some ways I want to keep her little for always, but I know she needs to grow up. Looking at her like this and thinking about what could have happened…" She closed her eyes, her chest tight. "I don't know how to thank you for bringing her home. She could have been gone forever, if not for you. I think she knows that, even as young as she is."

He turned her until she faced him then held her chin up with one finger.

"I would never have stopped looking for her. Never."

Karen raised her eyelids and looked into his blue, blue eyes. "I know that now and I'll never doubt you again, where the children are concerned."

"But you will where you are concerned?"

His voice, though still a whisper, was laced with ice.

"What can I do to convince you? I'm not the same man who pawed you before our wedding."

"I'm beginning to believe that, but it's only been a couple of weeks. How can I know that you've really changed in that short amount of time?"

"I understand and you're right. We've only been married a little while. I don't blame you for being cautious."

He let her go and grabbed his shirt, socks and boots.

"I'll go start the coffee."

Adam walked out of the room.

For some reason, she wanted to cry. Was she being too hard on him? He was making a concerted effort to be the kind of husband she wanted, but was his effort enough?

Chapter 15

Saturday came and along with it, Ben and Martha's wedding. Adam dressed in his best suit, actually his only suit, of black wool with a white shirt and black tie. He'd finally moved all of his clothes to Karen's house. Their closet nearly burst with all the clothes.

To Karen's hungry gaze, he looked spectacular. They hadn't made love yet. Always one thing or another kept them apart. Usually children, hers or those she delivered.

A baby boom was happening in Seattle, which was not unexpected. A lot of the brides who traveled from New Bedford had married, according to the original plan. As of now, more than a year after they arrived all the women were close and thought of themselves as sisters. Two of the dormitories sat empty as the remaining brides moved in order to be closer to their 'sisters'.

They all came to the wedding of one of their own, sweet Martha Haller. Karen wore her best dress, the same one that caused Adam to change into the jealous man that forced them to marry.

She turned in front of the cheval mirror shipped by her friend back in New Bedford. Her dress was still a little tight, though she'd lost weight since she'd married, and she didn't know how that could have happened since Adam was always making sure she ate.

Adam came up behind her.

"The infamous dress that caused my idiocy and got us hitched. Are you sure you want to wear that? I might go crazy again."

He slipped his hands around her waist and pulled her back against him.

"You know what this dress does to me. How am I to walk out of here in the state I'm in?"

She rubbed her bum against him and couldn't mistake his ardor.

"Just remember you are giving little Martha away. You're her father for the day or at least the ceremony. If that obligation doesn't work, button your coat, which will cover you."

"We could always—"

She pulled out of his arms and turned to face him. "No, we can't. We will, life will not always interfere, but you should get used to always being interrupted. My life is chaotic and sometimes I have little time for making love. Since you put the lock on the door, at least the children can't come in without knocking. I should have had one installed when I moved in, but I had no need at the time." *I didn't know my dreams would actually be fulfilled and I would be your wife.*

He cupped her face and leaned down to kiss her.

She waited, heart hammering, for his lips to touch hers.

"We are long past the need for a lock on that door and tonight, I'll make you mine."

His lips melded with hers, feasting on her, tongues meeting tongues, each pressing for advantage. Dueling, circling, mating.

Adam broke the kiss.

But Karen wasn't ready for it to end. She cupped the back of his head and brought him down for round two until finally she pulled back, gasping for air.

"You literally take my breath away."

He placed his forehead against hers.

"And you mine. I intend to do more than take your breath away tonight. I'll make you scream with pleasure again and again before I let you sleep."

Heat filled her cheeks. "I can only imagine, but I look forward to your attempts to do so."

He pulled back and gazed down, eyebrows drawn together.

"Didn't Douglas give you pleasure before he took his own?"

She shook her head. "He seemed to always be in a hurry. Though I enjoyed our lovemaking, sometimes his was the only pleasure taken."

"Your dead husband was a terrible lover. I intend to show you what loving can be like between husband and wife."

She lifted an eyebrow. "I'd like that. I want to know why some wives are so happy and others have marriages that seem only bearable."

"Were you happy?"

"Yes and no. The fact that I was in love with Douglas before I married him helped and I think he might have cared for me as well." *I just realized I had ended up with the same situation with Adam. He doesn't love me, but he definitely cares. Is that enough this time?*

"Your eyes are suddenly sad. You're thinking of our situation and that we were forced to marry. But ours is a different marriage. I intend to make you happy. That is my only concern, well, you and the children."

Karen's heart ached. She was happy he cared, but why couldn't he be in love with her as she was with him. She reached up and slid her finger down his cheek. "I know and that is the only reason we are not annulling this marriage. You see, I care for you, too. We would have ended up married, I know that, but we would have had time to get to know one another better. I guess we still can. I want the long walks and picnics and candy."

He closed his eyes and leaned against her palm, and then he raised his head. "We'll talk more later. We should gather the children and go to the church. I can't be late."

The closeness she'd just felt was gone. In its place was the cool, collected man with a stiff demeanor that she didn't understand. Was it her imagination?

The church was packed. Both Martha and Ben were well liked, and every bride and lumberjack that could fit inside the church was there. Luckily the first row was reserved for the bride's family—Adam, Karen and the kids.

Adam's brothers and their wives and kids filled out the rest of that row and the one behind.

Martha's maid of honor was Alice Newcomb, Karen's friend who cared for the children while Karen worked.

Ben's best man was Sven Gunderson, a man as big as Ben who had eyes only for Alice. *That's nice*, thought Karen. *Alice needs a beau and it would appear Sven wants the position.*

The church held a standing-room-only audience when Mrs. Peabody began to play the "Bridal Chorus" from the opera *Lohengrin* by Richard Wagner.

The doors to the church ante-chamber opened, and Martha walked in on Adam's arm. She positively beamed, her smile lighting up her face. She wore a simple pink dress with matching jacket and hat that made her glow.

Martha nodded at just about everyone in the church, smiling as she passed.

Adam looked the part of a proud papa, and when Reverend Peabody asked who gives this woman, Adam's "I do" rang out loud and clear.

When he sat next to Karen he placed her hand in the crook of his elbow and covered it with his.

She looked up at him. He faced forward but a smile broke the hard planes of his square jaw. Why had she never noticed the little dimple next to the left side of his mouth? Or the crinkles at his eyes from being in the sun or from liking to smile?

"You're staring at me. Pay attention to the ceremony," he whispered out the side of his mouth.

She dutifully pulled her attention away from her handsome husband and back to the ceremony.

"Do you, Martha Haller, take this man to be your lawful wedded husband?" intoned Reverend Peabody.

"I do."

"Do you, Ben Bundy, take this woman to be your lawfully wedded wife?"

"I do."

"Then by the power vested in me, I pronounce you man and wife. You may kiss your bride."

Ben turned to Martha, lifted her chin with his finger and bent nearly in half to kiss her. Then he grasped her waist and lifted her as if she was no more than a child. She wrapped her arms around his neck and placed her lips on his.

Although where she found them in all that red beard, Karen couldn't imagine. She much preferred the clean shaven look that Adam and his brothers all wore.

The guests all clapped and the happy couple looked out over the crowd, big grins on both of them. Then Ben lowered Martha to the floor and they walked out of the church and on over to Dolly's saloon, where the brides had set up a reception.

Alice shyly took Sven's arm and they followed Ben and Martha.

Row by row the rest of the church emptied.

While they waited, Adam squeezed her hand.

"This wedding is the kind you wanted, isn't it?"

"This wedding is the kind every woman wants, but few get. Why do you ask?"

"If you wanted, we can renew our vows in a ceremony like this one. I won't deny you your dream wedding."

Karen leaned against his arm. "No need. We are married. Everyone important was there."

"My family are not the only important people who would attend our wedding. I'm sure you would have wanted the brides there, if they could have been."

"Perhaps. I'll think about it."

Adam stood and stepped to the end of the row so Karen could get out, then he held out his arm for her.

She placed her hand through the crook in his elbow and they walked down the aisle, the children following.

When they got to Dolly's, the reception was in full swing. Music was provided by the local three piece band—a violinist, cellist, and a piano. The floor in the middle of the room was clear of tables so people could dance.

Ben and Martha were out on the floor twirling to a waltz. The next dance was a Virginia reel, followed by another waltz.

Adam held his hand out to Karen.

"Care to dance with me, Mrs. Talbot?"

Karen smiled. The last time she'd danced was with Douglas before his last deployment. She took Adam's hand, and he led her to the edge of the dancers. There he took her in his arms, pulled her close and they whirled around the floor.

Adam was a good dancer. Much better than she was. He led her through the dance and when she would have sat, he shook his head.

"I'm not letting you go that easily."

He swung her back around to the rhythm of the dance.

About halfway through, Ethan tapped Adam on the shoulder.

"I'll cut in on this dance, please."

Adam stopped, turned and slowly, released her.

"One dance. That's all you get."

Ethan took Adam's place.

He pulled her close. "I've been trying to get you alone. I'd like to get to know you better." His hand moved lower to her bum. "I'm sure we could come to some sort of arrangement," he smirked.

Karen gasped, stopped moving and slapped him.

She looked around them and saw the dancers had all stopped and were gazing toward her and Ethan.

"You slimy snake." She squared her shoulders and lifted her chin. "How dare you proposition me? I'm a married woman and faithful wife."

Ethan turned beet red, looked around and hunched his shoulders.

"Keep your voice down. You're attracting attention."

Her heart pounded in her chest and her pulse raced. "I don't care. Everyone here should know what kind of man...no, boy...that you are. Grow up, Ethan."

She turned and walked into a solid wall. Looking up, she saw Adam. His mouth a thin line, his eyebrows bunched together and his eyes were practically slits. His top lip curled back into a snarl.

"Ethan. Outside. Now."

Ethan held up his hands.

"Look I was just making a jest. No harm was done."

Adam moved around Karen so she was behind him.

He obviously didn't buy his explanation.

"If you don't go outside, I'll flatten you right here. Either way, you'll feel my fist in your pretty face. You won't be so pretty with a broken nose."

"No, look, I—"

Whatever he would have said was cut off by Adam's fist hitting him squarely on his nose. She remembered his story of his father beating them and him not wanting to be that way, however, in this instance, a solid punch was needed.

Blood spattered under both sides of Adam's fist and the crunch of broken cartilage was heard loud and clear.

Ethan put a hand on his nose and raised the other.

"Oww. No more. I'm leaving."

He ran out of the saloon.

Adam turned to Karen.

"Are you all right?"

"I'm fine. You really didn't have to hit him."

"I really did. He had it coming for a long time. He's a spoiled brat and always has been. Maybe now he'll think twice before he propositions another man's wife."

"I don't know. He seems to be a slow learner, you've already had to hit him for lusting after me.

Let me look at your hand." She looked at his right hand, still in a fist. "Relax. You're covered in blood."

"His."

"Nevertheless, we should get you cleaned up. Let's go home. We've made spectacles of ourselves and ruined the Bundy's reception. That's enough for one day."

They walked out of the reception.

"I'm not sorry I hit him." He sighed. "But I am sorry I didn't just drag him outside to do it."

"It's all right." She paused and then spoke softly. "Thank you for standing up for my honor."

Adam stopped walking. "I will fight for you every time. You're my wife. No one insults you. Not even someone purported to be my family."

She dropped her gaze to the ground and clasped her hands in front of her. Then she looked directly into his eyes.

"No one has ever fought for me before. I've always fought my own battles. Even when I was married to Douglas, he was never there to argue with the landlord or the bank or whoever. I had to do that. I'm not used to depending on anyone. So, thank you." She licked her lips and then smiled. "I should have punched him myself."

Adam laughed. "My delicate flower."

Karen chuckled. "Not so delicate after all."

He took his left hand and lifted her chin, then kissed her.

"Shall we continue?" he asked when he broke the kiss.

"I think we should. You know...the children will be occupied with the games in the reception for a couple more hours. If you want we could, you know."

He leaned down and kissed her forehead whispering, "I want more than a couple of hours. I want all night."

Karen felt the heat of his words directly in her womanly center. She'd never wanted anyone, like she wanted Adam Talbot.

When they got to the house, she made Adam wash his hands and then examined them for scrapes, cuts, and broken bones. He had none, so she kissed his knuckles.

"My knight in shining armor."

"I'm just the man who had your music box repaired. No knight here."

"You did do that for me. Brought music back into the house. I love you for that." Eyes wide, she slapped a hand over her mouth. "I mean...I... thank, yes thank you for that."

He lifted an eyebrow.

"Love. You said love...you can't take it back."

She closed her eyes, her stomach clenched.

Dear Lord, what have I done?

CHAPTER 16

Adam grinned. "You love me. I like that."

Karen raised her chin and straightened her back. "It's just a saying. Using that phrase is simply a way of saying a personal thank you."

His grin never faltered. "I don't believe you. If it was just a phrase, you wouldn't have clasped your hand over your mouth or looked shocked that you said it."

She cleaned up the mess and set her supplies straight. "Even if you're right, what difference does it make? You don't love me, so the point is moot."

At her words, the grin left his face.

"If it was possible, you're the only woman I could love. I want you to know that. I care for you very much, and the kids...they are wonderful. I look forward to having children with you. You make beautiful babies."

She couldn't deny that. Her children were beautiful—the best looking children in town. But, of course, she was a bit prejudiced. Thinking of them, she smiled. He knew just how to get her to smile and forget her disappointment, even anger.

"Adam, I want to make love to you. I want to consummate our marriage. Now. Not later. We can be together again tonight, but I want you now."

His smile returned.

"I'm very glad you want to make love as much as I want you, but," he cupped her face with his hand. "Tonight is soon enough. You may be called out for a birthing or some other thing today."

She shook her head. "I won't be. Everyone thinks I'm at the wedding reception for the afternoon and they—"

Someone pounded on the front door.

She and Adam both looked in the direction of the sound.

Adam cocked a brow. "You were saying?"

Karen took a deep breath, and then headed to the door. She heard a baby crying on the other side and wrenched the door open.

Paul and Genny Petersen were on the porch. Their mouths were turned down and their brows wrinkled.

"Mrs. Talbot, it's our little Grace," said Paul.

He looked down at the bundle his wife held. Their daughter, Grace, was screaming at the top of her little lungs.

Genny looked up at Karen, tears filling her unusual gray eyes. "We don't know what to do. Please help us."

Karen held her arms out for the baby. "Give her to me so I can examine her."

Genny gave the baby to Karen who carried her to the kitchen.

Grace isn't overly hot. "Adam, please lay a towel on the table for me."

He grabbed a bath towel from the pantry folded it in half and laid it on the table.

Karen placed Grace on the towel and opened her blanket. Then she stripped the baby of the little white gown and diaper she wore. She checked the umbilical cord and found that it had dried and fallen off and her navel wasn't infected.

"Did you know this diaper is soaking wet and she's also sitting in her bowel movement. How often do you change her?"

"Twice a day," responded Paul.

Karen closed her eyes and counted to five. She was certain the parents would be frightened if she counted to ten. *I really must talk to more parents about their experience with babies.*

"You need to change her every time she pees which should be about every hour during the day and every time she wakes to be nursed during the night."

Genny gasped, her eyes wide.

Paul's eyes widened and he shook his head. "We don't have that many diapers and we can't afford to buy more."

"Use hand towels, cut up a sheet, do whatever you have to. During the day you can leave her naked, but then you'll have to clean whatever she is laying on."

Karen wasn't surprised by the flaming red rash covering Grace's genitals, front and back, right down to the tops of her thighs.

She took the baby to the sink and looked over at Adam. "Would you pour some water from the tea kettle into the dish pan?"

He headed to the stove to do her bidding. "Don't you want me to heat it first?"

"No, it will be warm enough and this little one will probably appreciate the coolness. And would you go into the kids room and bring me the 'new baby package' I have there. You'll recognize it because of the pink ribbon it's tied with."

As soon as he walked away with the kettle, Karen placed the suffering baby in the pan and splashed water over her bottom.

"You see what I'm doing? She needs a bath at the very least once per day. With the state of her little body right this minute, you should give her a bath at least twice per day. And you need to thoroughly clean her every time you change her diaper and sprinkle corn starch on her, front and back. It will help keep her dry and protect her skin."

"We didn't know," said Genny, tears trailing down her cheeks. "Paul and I are both only children so we never saw how to care for a baby."

Karen stomped down her anger and calmed herself. The emotions she felt would do no one any good.

"Grace will be fine, but she'll need special care. I'll write you instructions."

Paul cleared his throat. "Neither of us knows how to read."

"Okay, you'll just have to remember. You must keep her clean and dry. I'm giving you some salve which you can put on her each time you change her diaper. Use a thin coat. Don't put too much on, it will just make a mess. More is not better."

She showed them just how to do it.

"Launder the diapers every day and make sure she is as clean and dry as possible."

Genny took a now happy Grace from Karen.

"Until that rash is gone you must change her every time she pees or poops. You have to be diligent and check her, though given the look of her little bottom, she'll let you know because she'll hurt. You should carry at least one clean diaper with you all the time. Being away from home is no excuse."

Genny smiled. "Thanks, Mrs. Talbot. Thanks so much. You must think us the worst parents you've ever seen."

Grace's happy for probably the first time in days, thought Karen. *That poor baby.* "No, not the worst. You didn't know any better but you love your daughter. I've seen the situation where that is not the case."

Genny's eyes widened. "Someone did that to their child on purpose?"

"They just didn't care enough to put in the effort needed to care for a baby, and the baby is the one who suffered. The situation was very sad and criminal in my book."

Genny nodded, her eyes welling with more tears. "I totally agree. I can't imagine not caring. I love Grace so much. The fact that I was so stupid and didn't come to you sooner makes me sick. I never wanted to cause her pain."

Karen put her arm around Genny. "I know that. There is no permanent harm done. Her little bottom will clear up in no time if you care for her as I've instructed."

Genny looked down at Grace, lying peacefully in Genny's arms, and then to Paul, who had tears in his eyes, too.

"We're gonna raise her right, and if we have any more questions or think we might be doing something wrong, we'll come to you right away."

Karen squeezed Genny's shoulders before letting her go. "That's wonderful. I'm always here to help you."

"What do we owe you?" asked Paul.

Karen could tell he was dreading the answer. She also knew they had no money.

"You don't owe me a thing. This visit is considered follow-up birthing care. Just take care of Grace. That's all the payment I require."

Paul's face split in to a grin, revealing yellowing, crooked teeth.

"Thank you, Mrs. Talbot. Thank you very much."

Adam returned with the birthing gift.

Karen had two pair of knitted soakers, a dozen diapers, safety pins, a gown and a bath towel. The items cost her just over two-dollars at the mercantile.

She escorted them to the front door and bid them farewell before returning to the kitchen.

When she returned, Adam was seated at the table, his long legs stretched out in front of him.

"You were saying? No one would come for you today?"

She threw up her hands, closed her eyes and took a deep breath. "All right. I was wrong. But, don't you see? That is the way our life is always going to be. I lead a life that can't be planned or timed. We have to take the opportunities as they arise."

Adam went to where she stood in the middle of the floor.

"I can see that now. I will stop trying to plan when to be together."

He cupped her face.

"We'll just take the times that we have. Now, how long until the kids come home?"

Karen gazed up at her husband. His blue eyes stood out in sharp contrast to the tan of his skin. She'd discovered he was tanned down to the waist, demonstrating he worked under the sun without his shirt. She couldn't imagine watching him, seeing his muscles flex with his efforts and not wanting him right then and there. Those feelings were similar to what she felt now.

She shook her head. "Too soon."

"Do you want to go back to the reception?"

She closed her eyes and sighed. "No. I just want to get out of this dress and into one that's more comfortable."

"You don't like your dress? But I thought—"

She put two fingers over his soft, firm lips. "I know what you thought, but it is the only dress I have that hasn't yet seen better days."

She removed her fingers. "The only male I want to entice is you. I don't care right now whether you love me or not. You love my children and that will have to do."

Looking up, she saw him smile and his eyes twinkled.

"I'm glad you love me. I didn't want to be the only one in this relationship with those feelings."

Her mouth dropped open and her heart skipped a beat. "You...you're...in love with me? How long have you known?"

When he didn't say anything, she pounded on his chest. "How long have you made me suffer?"

He took both her hands in his.

"I never wanted you to suffer. I tried to deny my feelings for so long, but when you delivered Grace, when you cared about Paul's feelings when he paid you and when you took care of Grace just now I knew. I realized I had for a long time, even before I started to court you. But I denied it because I didn't want to be hurt."

She moved her hand and he let her go. She cupped his face then slid a hand around to the back of his neck and pulled him down to kiss her.

"I would never hurt you. I've loved you for so very long and then when you fixed my music box, my heart nearly burst with my love. That you would take the time to do something like that for my children—for me—I knew what a special man you are."

She whispered against his lips. "I want to make a baby, my love, as soon as possible. I want lots of babies with you. You're an amazing father."

"Tonight. I want to show you just how much I love you."

"I can't wait for tonight. We might as well go back to the reception and make sure that with us gone they aren't bothering Alice, so Sven can talk to her."

"Sven?"

She nodded. "He had eyes only for her throughout the ceremony and smiled wide when she placed her arm around the crook of his elbow. He looked so proud. I expect them to be the next to get married."

He tilted his head for a moment. "They did make a handsome couple. We'll have to build some more houses. The men are finding brides much faster now that the women have been here for more than a year."

"I like the fact that Talbot Lumber builds a small house for each new couple. Giving them a home to start out with, is so nice. I wouldn't have my house if not for your company."

He shrugged.

"Not really. We want to give them the best start possible. We want them to stay here and work for us. We want them to have children and help Seattle grow. So, you see, our reasons are totally selfish."

"Whatever the reason, it's a wonderful gesture."

"I'm glad you think so. Now, let's go get our children."

She loved the fact he thought of Larry and Patty as his children, too. The gesture warmed her deep inside.

When they arrived back at the reception, all of Adam's brothers and their families surrounded them.

Jason walked close and clapped Adam on the shoulder.

"That was a good hit you gave Ethan. He's had it coming for…oh…about ten years."

All of them laughed.

"Why did we put up with him this long?" asked Michael.

"He's family." Jason shrugged. "Mother would have had our hides if we'd done anything to harm her perfect nephew. She never knew, or at least refused to see, what kind of person he really was. When he showed up this time, I'd hoped he'd changed. He hadn't. As a matter of fact, I think he's gotten worse."

Ethan approached the group, his nose no longer bleeding.

"Adam. Karen. I'm sorry for the way I acted. I was completely out of line, and Adam was right to knock some sense in me. I'm jealous of what you all have found. I'll be leaving on the next ship headed to San Francisco and staying at the Seattle Inn until then."

He held out a hand to Adam.

"Can you forgive me?"

Adam accepted his hand and shook it. "I'm not the one who you need to apologize to." He tilted his head toward Karen.

"Of course." He turned toward her. "Karen, can you forgive me my boorish behavior? I've always gotten what I wanted when I wanted it whether it was a new suit or a woman's affections. That is wrong of me and I will change my behavior. Actually, I want to marry some day, but I won't find a wife until I make myself a better man. You and Adam have started me on that road. Thank you."

He held out a hand out.

When she put her hand in his he brought it to his lips and kissed the top.

I doubt very seriously his change in attitude will last long. Someone who has been indulged his whole life can't change overnight. "I forgive you, Ethan. You have a lot of work ahead of you if you really want to marry. But it would appear you are on the right path. I wish you good luck."

"Thank you. That means a lot to me."

He turned and left the reception.

Adam turned to the group and grinned. "If I'd known punching him in the nose would set him on the straight and narrow, I'd have done it years ago."

His brothers laughed. His sisters-in-law smiled.

Karen laughed and shook her head.

"That's my husband. Always willing to help a family member."

Adam wrapped his arms around her waist and kissed her soundly. When he pulled back, he whispered, "I love you, you know that?"

She reached up and ran her thumb across his cheek. Stubble was already forming and tickled her palm. Then she cupped his jaw. "I know. I love you back."

The family clapped.

Karen and Adam gazed over at all the smiling faces.

Jason put his arm around Adam's shoulders.

"Think love doesn't exist now, little brother?"

Adam shook his head. "I'm much smarter now. I was an idiot when I said those words."

"You were. I'm glad you found out before it was too late."

"I wasn't entirely wrong." He looked down into Karen's upturned face. "A little lust doesn't hurt, either."

Karen grinned and her heart soared. She was looking more than a little forward to the night to come.

CHAPTER 17

Adam surprised Karen by asking Jason if the kids could spend the night.

"Of course," said Rachel, holding Abbie. "Anytime. Billy is really good with them and enjoys playing with the kids. They like watching Abbie, too, but they get a little bored since she's not big enough to play with them yet."

"We'll return the favor," promised Adam.

Jason nodded. "I'll remember that the next time I want to take my lady wife to Olympia on a shopping trip."

"We'll bring by the kids pajamas and clothes for tomorrow, later."

"That's fine," said Rachel.

Adam said their goodbyes to his family while Karen gathered Larry and Patty.

When he found her, she was explaining the situation to them.

She knelt in front of them. "How would you two like to spend the night at Uncle Jason's and Aunt Rachel's tonight?"

"Yes. Yay!" shouted Larry, shooting a fist in the air. "I'll get to play with Billy all night."

"No," said Karen, with a sigh. "You still have to go to bed at your regular time."

Larry pouted for a moment and then smiled.

Karen narrowed her eyes. "What are you planning?"

"Nothing. Are we sleeping in Billy's room?"

Karen raised an eyebrow and shook her head at the little schemer. "I'll make sure that you and Patty stay in Daddy's old room, where you can't get into any trouble."

"Ah, Mama, you're no fun."

She wrapped her arms around him and kissed him on the cheek. "I'm your mama; I'm not supposed to be fun. I'm supposed to do my best to see that you are raised right and become a good man, like your daddy." She looked up at Adam and smiled.

He hadn't realized she knew he stood behind her.

Larry looked up at Adam.

"Will I be like you someday? I want to climb trees and watch them fall. I want to be a lumberjack."

Adam tousled the boy's hair.

"I'll see that you learn how to climb trees and a whole lot of other things. The world is a big place, and you and Patty will need every advantage we can give you to live in it well. Now, kiss your mother and give me a hug before you go with Uncle Jason."

Larry dutifully kissed Karen and hugged Adam. Patty did the same.

Jason held his hand out to Larry and picked up Patty before walking out the door.

Adam gazed down at Karen. "Are you ready to leave?"

He was finally about to make love to his wife. Hopefully, they wouldn't get interrupted again.

Karen's life was chaotic. Would he be able to accept that fact?

Heart hammering in her chest, she nodded. "I'm more than ready."

He leaned down and whispered so no one else would hear. "You're not quite ready, but you will be, I'll make sure of it."

Heat flooded her cheeks and she dropped her chin.

Adam laughed.

He liked to tease her and he was good at it.

He grabbed her hand and led them through the crowd. After they got outside, he sped up, practically dragging her along. Now that they had the time, he was like a schoolboy with a new toy…he couldn't wait to try it out.

They reached home, and Adam pulled her through the door. He kissed her hard and swept her up into his arms, kicking the door closed behind them. Then his long strides made short work of the distance to the bedroom.

He set her on her feet and started to undress.

Karen walked to the bed and lit the lamp on the nightstand. "Adam, slow down. We have all night."

"No, we don't as that visit from the Petersen's proved. We don't know when you'll be called on to help someone, and I intend to make the best use of the time we have. As you wanted, this first time will be hard and fast."

Shaking her head, she stepped back. "I don't want it that way now. I want you to show me how you'll make me ready. You said you would."

He stopped unbuttoning his trousers, and his hands dropped to his sides.

"I'm being an oaf, aren't I?"

Karen clasped her hands in front of her. "A little."

"Very well, I'll show you just how much I love you. We'll take it slow. Get to know each other's likes and dislikes."

He walked over and wrapped his arms around her, trapping her hands in between their bodies.

She looked up at him, eyes wide.

Adam leaned down and kissed her.

Karen squirmed wanting to free her hands to wrap them around his neck, but he just held her tighter.

"I'll make you scream my name," he promised.

Stepping back, he released her but didn't let her go far. He unbuttoned her dress and slid it down her shoulders into a puddle on the floor.

"Have I told you women wear too many clothes?"

She lifted an eyebrow. "No, you hadn't mentioned it." *I don't want to know how he knows that.*

Undoing every hook on her corset in no time, he let it drop on top of the dress. The corset was followed by her chemise and her bloomers.

She still wore her stockings, tied with blue ribbon above her knee.

"I like the stockings. Let's leave them on...for now."

"All right."

He reached up to unbutton his shirt but she pushed his hands aside.

Now it was her turn.

"I want to undress you."

She unbuttoned his shirt and pushed it down his arms off onto the floor. Then she started to undo his pants where he had left off, but he still had his boots on.

"Sit on the bed, please. I need to remove your boots."

Dutifully he did as she said.

She turned her back to him, put his leg between hers and tugged the tall leather boot off. Then she did the same thing with the other foot.

"There. You can stand now."

He did and reached for his pants.

Grinning, she batted his hands away.

"I want to."

She pushed them over his slim hips and down his legs until he had to step out of them. He was glorious. as she'd seen from the glances she took.

Gasping at the sight, she stood.

"I don't scare you do I?" She heard the vulnerability in his voice.

"No. You're a beautiful man. More so than I had believed. But scare me? No. You forget I'm a midwife, nearly a doctor, and I know how everything fits together. Besides that, I've been married and had children. You don't frighten me in the least. You're just *more* than I expected, that I don't deny."

His smile spread across his face.

He was even more attractive to her with his smile, if that was possible.

She took his hand and led him back to their bed. At the edge, she pulled back the blankets and the top sheet to the bottom of the bed. Then she scooted to the middle and lay down.

Karen held up her arms in welcome.

Adam came down beside her and leaned on his elbow. He stared at her.

She remembered Douglas only liked making love one way, missionary style. What if she wasn't adventurous enough?

He kissed her lips, then her neck and the hollow at the base of her neck. He went lower to her breasts, teasing the nipples with his teeth and then soothing with his tongue.

Karen had never felt anything like this. Douglas insisted they make love in the dark, and he'd never kissed her breasts much less taken them into his mouth. This was a new sensation, different than nursing children. Feeding her children never sent waves of desire rolling through her to settle in her core.

Adam moved lower, pleasuring her with his mouth and fingers until finally she did scream his name.

After she settled, he spread her legs and positioned himself above her, and then he made love to her. Sweet, complete love. Considering where she was in her cycle, she wouldn't be surprised to find they had made a baby tonight.

After he was done, he rolled to his back taking her with him.

She cuddled into his side, content. She'd never been made love to like he had just done.

Karen rested her cheek on Adam's chest with her arm across his stomach.

"That was amazing. I'm exhausted and feel like a rag doll left in the rain."

Adam chuckled and wrapped an arm around her.

"I hope you're not too tired. Round two will be coming up."

Wide-eyed, she lifted her head and looked at him. "Round two?"

"After all this time, you didn't think once would be enough, now did you?"

Her heart raced. "Well, I—"

He grazed her cheek with his thumb.

"Once will never be enough with you."

He pulled her on top of him and then eased her head down for a kiss.

"Nope, never enough."

They made love long into the night until both were so spent that sleep was the only thing they could do.

As she shut her eyes, once again in his embrace, held to his side with one big arm over her, she smiled. Life turned out to be grander than she'd ever hoped for. She found a man she loved and who loved her in return. One who loved her children and cared for them as his own.

Tears leaked from her eyes onto his chest.

He raised his head and looked at her.

"Why are you crying? Are you unhappy?"

The concern in his voice touched her.

"Just the opposite. I'm very happy. More so than I ever believed possible."

"Then why are you crying?"

She ran her fingers through the light sprinkling of hair on his chest, watching it curl around them. "Because I am so happy."

He laid his head back down.

"I don't think I'll ever understand women."

"All you have to understand is that I love you and always will."

"That I understand. I love you, too."

He rubbed a hand over her back, soothing her to sleep. Perchance to dream.

Epilogue

Nine and one half months later

Karen lay in their bed in the new house. Adam built a two-story log house on land near Jason. They'd turned her old house into the clinic she wanted, but she wouldn't be seeing patients for a few weeks. She had one of her newborn babies at her breast and the second lying next to her.

Adam walked in from downstairs, picked up the baby on the bed and then lay down next to Karen.

"Libby's sleeping. She must have been the first to nurse."

Karen nodded. "She was awake and fussing. Her brother couldn't be bothered to wake up. Even now, I have to keep waking him so he'll eat."

"Sounds like he takes after his cousin Billy. It's hell getting that boy up in the mornings."

"How are Larry and Patty this morning?" She shifted, preparing to get up. "I should be up fixing their breakfast."

"You stay in bed with our youngest babies, and I'll take care of the older ones. I am quite a good cook, you know."

Karen chuckled, remembering the first time he'd brought her food while they were courting. "Yes, I know. You've proven again and again how good your food is. I'm very lucky to have married a man with your skills."

He voice deepened and he lifted an eyebrow. "I'm not only skilled in the kitchen."

"I know." She waved her hand over the babies. "These two are the result of your skill in the bedroom."

Libby's face crinkled in a definite frown and Karen was sure she would wake, but she didn't. She relaxed and stayed asleep.

"I would bet our daughter just made a mess in her diaper, and you, Daddy, get to change her."

"But she's sleeping. I'd hate to wake her."

Karen frowned. "I don't want her sitting in the waste. You know it won't take but a minute and if she does wake, you'll get to walk the floor and put her back to sleep."

"All right. I'll change her, but I won't like it."

"But you'll do it because you love me...and her. You don't want her little bum to get red and sore."

Adam stood, his baby daughter in his arms still asleep.

"She woke up."

Karen smiled. "Oh good. I love watching her make bubbles when she's awake. She's so cute. They both are."

He leaned over and kissed her.

"You just want me to stay up here with you. But you know I can't. The other two kids need to eat and then they'll want to come see the babies."

"Then I guess you better hurry and change her diaper."

"Guess I better get to it."

He laid Libby on the bed and retrieved a diaper and wet washrag.

"This water is barely lukewarm. She won't like it very much."

"Good thing you'll be quick."

After Adam changed Libby, he laid her back down next to Karen.

"I'll return after I feed Larry and Patty."

"We'll be here waiting with bated breath." She pulled baby Eric from her nipple and put him to her shoulder to burp.

He still looked asleep, but she didn't want him waking up later with a tummy ache, so she kept patting his back until he burped and spit up on the tea towel over her shoulder.

"Do you think you have time to lie with us before you feed the kids?"

"I always have time to lie with you. Besides, they are still in bed. I have to get them up to eat breakfast."

He got on the bed and scooted next to Karen after picking up Libby again. Adam stretched his long, long legs in front of him and laid Libby on his thighs then raised his knees so he could see her face.

"Hello, baby girl. How is my sweet girl?"

Libby smiled and blew a bubble.

"Did you see that? She smiled when I talked to her."

Karen laughed. "That was gas. They are too young to smile for something we say."

"Believe what you want. I say she smiled. Isn't that right, Libby? You smiled at Daddy."

The infant blinked her big blue eyes, surrounded by long black lashes and smiled again.

"See? Did you see that? She smiled again. I'm telling you, she knows who her daddy is."

Karen rolled her eyes. "Whatever you say." She laid her head on Adam's shoulder and closed her eyes for a moment. Exhaustion was nearly overtaking her.

Adam turned his head and kissed Karen's forehead.

"Hmm. I love you. I just need a minute. I'd forgotten how hard life is with newborns."

"I love you, too. Always."

He leaned over, kissed her lips.
She smiled. Life was good.

ABOUT THE AUTHOR

CYNTHIA WOOLF is the award winning and best-selling author of twenty-five historical western romance books and two short stories with more books on the way.

Cynthia loves writing and reading romance. Her first western romance, *Tame A Wild Heart,* was inspired by the story her mother told her of meeting Cynthia's father on a ranch in Creede, Colorado. Although *Tame A Wild Heart* takes place in Creede that is the only similarity between the stories. Her father was a cowboy not a bounty hunter and her mother was a nursemaid (called a nanny now) not the ranch owner. The ranch they met on is still there as part of the open space in Mineral County in southwestern Colorado.

Writing as CA Woolf, she has six sci-fi, space opera romance titles. She calls them westerns in space.

Cynthia credits her wonderfully supportive husband Jim and her critique partners for saving her sanity and allowing her to explore her creativity.

WEBSITE – http://cynthiawoolf.com
NEWSLETTER – http://bit.ly/1qBWhFQ